“We are still married,”

Dracco reminded her. “Our marriage was never annulled.”

Imogen’s face cleared. “You want an annulment?” She ignored the stab of pain biting into her heart and concentrated instead on clinging to the relief she wanted to feel. “Well, of course, I will agree and—”

“No, I don’t want an annulment.” Dracco cut across her hurried assent. “Far from it. What I want is a *child*.”

Legally wed,
Great together in bed,
But he's never said...
"I love you."
They're...

The Harlequin Presents® series
in which marriages are made in haste...
and love comes later....

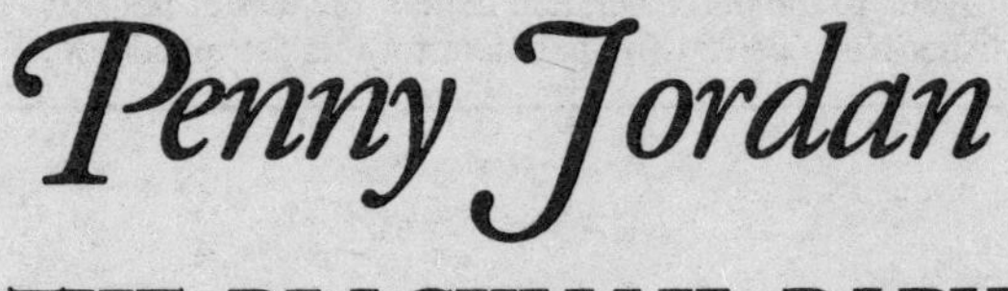

THE BLACKMAIL BABY

TORONTO • NEW YORK • LONDON
AMSTERDAM • PARIS • SYDNEY • HAMBURG
STOCKHOLM • ATHENS • TOKYO • MILAN • MADRID
PRAGUE • WARSAW • BUDAPEST • AUCKLAND

ISBN 0-373-12247-0

THE BLACKMAIL BABY

First North American Publication 2002.

This edition published by arrangement with Harlequin Books S.A.

Visit us at www.eHarlequin.com

Printed in U.S.A.

PROLOGUE

'SO YOU'RE going to go through with it? You're going to go ahead and marry Dracco, even though he doesn't love you?'

Imogen flinched as the full venom of her stepmother Lisa's words hit her. They were in Imogen's bedroom, or at least the bedroom that had been Imogen's until after her father's death. Since then Lisa had declared her intention to sell the pretty country house where Imogen had grown up and to buy herself a modern apartment in the small market town where they lived.

'Dracco has asked me to be on hand to help him entertain the clients,' Lisa had said at the time of her shock announcement about the house. 'He says he can see how much more business the company has been attracting since I became your father's hostess. Unfortunately your mother never seemed to realise just how vitally important being a good hostess was.'

She had given the openly dismissive, almost contemptuous shrug with which Imogen had become teeth-grittingly familiar whenever Lisa spoke about her late mother. Instinctively Imogen had wanted to leap to her mother's defence, but she had sufficient experience of Lisa to know better than to do so. Even so, she had not been able to stop herself from pointing out quietly, 'Mummy was ill. Otherwise, I know she would have wanted to entertain Daddy's clients for him.'

'Oh, yes, we all know that you think your precious mother was a saint.' Imogen had seen the furious look of hostility in Lisa's hard blue eyes. 'And Dracco agrees with me that you made life very difficult for your father all these years by constantly harping on about your mother, trying to make him feel guilty because he fell in love with me.'

Lisa had preened herself openly, making Imogen's stomach churn with sickening misery and anguish. Then her stepmother had continued triumphantly, 'Dracco considers that your father was very fortunate to be married to me. In fact...' She had stopped, giving Imogen a small, secret little smile that had made her heart thump heavily against her ribs. It hurt, unbearably, to hear Lisa speaking about Dracco as though a special closeness existed between them, especially when Imogen was so desperately in love with him herself!

Imogen had never truly been able to understand how her beloved father had fallen in love with a woman as cold and manipulative as Lisa. Granted, she was stunningly attractive: tall, blonde-haired, with a perfect and lushly curved body, totally unlike Imogen's own. Imogen took after her mother, who had been petite and fine-boned with the same thick dark mop of untameable blackberry curls and amazingly coloured dark violet eyes. And, where Imogen remembered her mother's eyes shining with warmth and love, Lisa's pale blue eyes were always cold.

Imogen had loved her father far too much, though, to say anything to him. Her mother had died when she was seven, and when he'd decided to remarry when she was fourteen Imogen had made up her mind to accept her new stepmother for his sake. She had adored her father and been fiercely protective of him, in her little-girl way, after her mother's death, but she had been ready to welcome into their lives anyone who could make him happy.

Lisa, though, had quickly made it plain that she was not prepared to be equally generous. She had been thirty-two when she married Imogen's father, with no particular fondness for children and even less for other members of her own sex. Right from the start of their relationship she had treated the young girl as an adversary, a rival for Imogen's father's affections and loyalty.

Lisa had been in their lives less than three months when she had told Imogen coolly that she considered it would be far better for her to go to boarding school than live at home and attend the local private school her mother had chosen before succumbing to the degenerative illness which had ultimately killed her. It had been Dracco who had stepped in then, reminding Imogen's father that his first wife had hand-picked her daughter's secondary school even when she knew she would not be alive to see Imogen attend it. It had been Dracco too who had come to that same school to break the news of her father's fatal accident to Imogen, tears sheening the normally composed and unreadable jade depths of his eyes.

That had been nearly twelve months ago. Imogen had been seventeen then, now she was eighteen, and in less than an hour's time she would be Dracco's wife.

The car that was to take her to the same small church where her parents had been married and her mother was buried was waiting outside. Inside it was her father's elderly solicitor, who was to give her away. It was to be a quiet wedding. She had pleaded fervently with Dracco for that.

So you're going to go through with it? You're going to go ahead and marry Dracco, even though he doesn't love you? Imogen's mind returned to her stepmother's deliberately painful question.

'Dracco says it's...it's for my own good...and that it's what my father would have wanted,' she answered.

"'Dracco says,''' Lisa Atkins mimicked cruelly. 'You are such a fool, Imogen. There is only one reason Dracco is marrying you and that's because of who you are. Because he wants to gain full control of the business.'

'No, that isn't true!' Imogen protested frantically. 'Dracco already runs the business,' she reminded her stepmother. 'He knows I would never try to change that.'

'*You* might not,' Lisa agreed coolly. 'But what about the man you may one day marry if Dracco doesn't step in? He may have other plans. Your father's will leaves your share in trust for you until you are thirty unless you marry before then. Oh, come on, Imogen. Surely you don't actually think that Dracco wants you?' One elegant eyebrow arched mockingly before Lisa went on, 'Dracco is a man! To him you are just a child, less than that, in fact... Dracco wants what you can give him. He has told me himself that if it wasn't for the business there is no way he'd be marrying you.'

Although she tried to stop herself, Imogen could not quite prevent the sharp gasp of pain escaping. She could see Lisa's triumphant smile, and hated herself for letting the older woman break through her defences.

In an effort to recover the ground she had lost, she began unsteadily, 'Dracco wouldn't—'

But she wasn't allowed to go any further; Lisa stopped her, saying softly, 'Dracco wouldn't what, Imogen? Dracco wouldn't confide in me? Oh, my dear, I'm afraid you are way behind the times. Dracco and I...' She paused and examined her perfectly manicured fingernails. 'Well, it should be for Dracco to tell you this and not me, but let us just say that Dracco and I have a relationship which is very special—to both of us.'

Imogen could hardly take in what she was being told. She felt sick with a numbing disbelief that this could be happening on her wedding day; the day that should have been one of the happiest of her life, but which now, thanks to Lisa's shocking revelations, was fast turning into one of the worst.

So far she had not given very much thought to the complexities of her father's will. She had been too grief-stricken by his loss to consider how his death would affect her financially. She knew, though, of course, that he had been an extremely successful and wealthy man. As an acclaimed financial adviser, John Atkins had been held in high esteem by both his clients and those he did business with. Imogen could still remember how enthusiastic and pleased he had been when he had first taken Dracco under his wing as a raw university graduate.

They had met when her father went to debate an issue at Dracco's university. Dracco had been on the opposing side and her father had been impressed not just by his debating skills but by his grasp of the whole subject, and what he had described as Dracco's raw energy and hunger to succeed.

Dracco had had a stormy childhood, abandoned by his own father and brought up by a succession of relatives after his mother had remarried and her second husband had refused to take him on. He had worked to pay his own way through university, and when he had first come to work for Imogen's father he had for a time lived with them.

It had been Dracco who had chauffeured her to school when her father was away on business; Dracco who had taught her to ride her new bike; Dracco the Dragon, as she had nicknamed him teasingly. And when her father had made him a junior partner in his business it had been Imogen Dracco had taken out to celebrate his promotion—to an ice-cream parlour in the local town.

Quite when her acceptance of him as Dracco, her father's partner and her own friend had changed, and she had begun to see him as Dracco, the man, Imogen wasn't sure.

She could remember coming out of school one day to find him waiting for her in the little scarlet sports car he had bought for himself. It had been a hot, sunny afternoon, the hood had been down, the sunlight glinting on the thick night-darkness of his hair. He had turned his head to look at her, as though sensing her presence even before she had reached him, and studied her with the intense dark greenness of his gaze.

Suddenly it had been as though she was seeing him for the first time. As though she had been struck by a thunderbolt. Her heart had started to race and then thud heavily.

She had felt sick, excited, filled with a dangerous, heady exuberance and a shocked self-consciousness.

Without knowing why, she had found that she wanted to look at his mouth. Somewhere deep inside her body an unfamiliar sensation had begun to uncurl itself; a sensation that had made her face blush bright red and her legs turn to jelly. She had felt as though she couldn't bear to be near him in case he guessed how she felt, but at the same time she couldn't bear him not to be there.

'Only a child as naïve and inexperienced as you could possibly think that Dracco wants you. A woman, a real woman, would know immediately that there was already someone else in his life. He hasn't even tried to take you to bed, has he?' Lisa challenged, before adding cruelly, 'And don't bother trying to pretend that you haven't wanted him to. That crush you have on him is painfully obvious.'

The sharp interruption of Lisa's goading voice broke into Imogen's thoughts. Instinctively she turned away from her stepmother to guard her expression, catching sight of her own reflection in the mirror as she did so. It had been Dracco who had insisted that she should wear a traditional wedding dress.

'Your father would have wanted you to,' had been his winning argument.

If there was one thing she and Dracco did share it was their mutual love for her father.

'Dracco doesn't love you. Not as a man loves a woman.'

Once again Imogen couldn't prevent a small sound of anguish escaping her lips.

Narrowing her eyes, Lisa dropped her voice to a soft, sensual purr. 'Surely even someone as sexless as you must have thought it odd that he hasn't taken you to bed? Any normal woman would guess immediately what that meant. Especially where an obviously red-blooded man like Dracco is concerned.' Lisa smiled unkindly at her. 'If you're determined to be an unwanted wife you will have to learn to conceal your feelings a little better. Surely you couldn't have imagined that there haven't been women in Dracco's life? He is, after all, a very potent man.'

Imogen prayed that she wouldn't be sick and that she wouldn't give in to her desire to run out of the room and away from Lisa's hateful, mocking voice. Of course she knew there had been other women in Dracco's life and she knew too what it felt like to be agonisingly jealous of them—after all, she had had enough practice.

Dracco with other girls; girls that he found attractive and desirable in all the ways he obviously did not view her; girls that he wanted in all the ways he did not want her, in his arms, in his bed, beneath the fierce male hardness of his body, naked, skin to skin, whilst he…

To Dracco she was nothing more than a baby, the daughter of his partner and closest friend, someone to be treated with amusement and paternalism as though twenty-odd years separated them and not a mere ten… Ten…a full decade… But soon they would be equals; soon now she would be Dracco's wife. Imogen gave a small shiver. All through her teenage years she had dreamed of her private fantasy coming true and of Dracco returning her love, telling her that he could not live without her, demanding passionately that she give herself to him and become his wife.

Of course, a tiny part of her, a voice she had refused out of fear and anguish to listen to, urged her to be cautious, to wonder why in all the things that Dracco had said to her since her father's death there had been no mention of love.

And somehow until now she had managed to ignore what that omission could mean. Until now.

There was, Imogen recognised through her shocked pain, an odd air of almost driven determination in her stepmother's manner, an air that bordered on furious desperation, but Imogen felt too weakened by her own anguish to consider why that might be.

Drawing herself up to her full height, she told Lisa with quiet dignity, 'Dracco is marrying me—'

'No,' Lisa told her furiously, 'Dracco is marrying your inheritance. Have you no pride, you little fool? Any woman worthy of the name would walk away now before it's too late, find herself a man who really wants her instead of crawling after one who doesn't; one who already has in his life the woman he really wants!'

Imogen felt as though she was inhabiting a nightmare. What further cruelty was Lisa trying to inflict on her? Whatever it was, she didn't want to hear it. She did not want to allow herself to hear it.

It was time for her to leave. Imogen started to walk past her stepmother but Lisa grabbed hold of her arm, stopping her, hissing viciously to her, 'I know what you're hoping but you're wasting your time; Dracco will never love you. He loves someone else. If you don't believe me, ask him! Ask him today, now, before he marries you, if there is someone; a woman in his life whom he loves. And ask him, if you dare, just who she is.'

* * *

A woman in Dracco's life whom he loved. Imogen's head was swimming with pain and fear as she started to walk down the aisle. She could see the back of Dracco's dark head as he waited for her to reach him. The scent of the lilies filling the church was so heady that it was making Imogen feel slightly sick and faint. How could that be true? How could he possibly even consider marrying her if he loved someone else?

Lisa had been lying… Lying, as she had done so often in the past, trying to cause trouble for Imogen; to hurt and upset her.

And as for her final comment, it had to be impossible, surely, as Lisa had been implying that she herself was the woman Dracco loved.

Totally, completely, unbearably impossible, at least so far as Imogen was concerned.

'Dearly beloved…'

Imogen felt herself start to sway. Immediately Dracco's fingers curled supportively around her arm.

Pain and longing filled her in equal measures. This should have been the happiest day of her life. She was, after all, marrying the man she loved. The man she had loved since she had first realised what love was.

'Imogen. Are you all right? For a moment in there I thought you were going to faint.'

Imogen tried to force a smile as she met the frowning concern in Dracco's gaze. Her husband's gaze. She could feel her knees threatening to buckle. She felt so odd. So…so alone and afraid.

'Dracco, there's something I want to ask you.'

They were standing outside the church whilst the bells pealed and their wedding guests chattered happily.

'Mmmm...'

Dracco was barely even looking at her, Imogen recognised miserably. They didn't seem like a newly married couple at all...like husband and wife, a pair of lovers. A sharp pain seemed to pierce her to her heart. Before she could lose her courage she demanded unevenly, 'Have you...? Is there...is there someone...a woman you love?'

He was looking at her now, Imogen recognised bitterly, concentrating all his attention on her, but not in the way she had longed for. He was frowning forbiddingly in the tense silence her nervous question had created.

Imogen could hardly bear to continue looking at him. She saw the flash of emotion glitter in the jade depths of his eyes; heard the furious anger in his voice as he demanded curtly, 'Who told you about that?'

Her heart felt as though it was breaking. It was true.

In numb despair she watched as he cursed grimly under his breath and then said more gently, 'Yes. Yes, there is. But...'

Dracco loved another woman. He loved another woman but he had still married her.

Imogen felt as though her whole world had come crashing down around her. Where was the man she had put on a pedestal; adored, trusted, loved? He didn't exist...

With a low cry of torment she turned on her heel and started to run, desperate to escape from her pain, from her stepmother's knowing triumph, but most of all from

Dracco himself, who had betrayed her and everything she had believed about him. Behind her she could hear Dracco calling her name, but that only made her run even faster. In the street beyond the church a taxi was pulling up to disgorge its passenger, and without stopping to think what she was doing Imogen ran up to it and jumped in. At any other time the way the taxi driver was goggling at her would have made her giggle, but laughing was the last thing she felt like doing right now…

'Quick,' she instructed the driver, her voice trembling. 'Please hurry.'

As she spoke she darted a quick backward glance towards the church, half expecting to see Dracco coming in pursuit of her, but the street behind her was empty.

'Don't tell me,' the taxi driver quipped jovially as he took in both his passenger's bridal array and her breathless anxiety, 'you're in a hurry to get to a wedding—right?' Laughing at his own joke, he started to negotiate the traffic.

'Wrong,' Imogen corrected him fiercely. 'I'm actually in a hurry to get away from one.'

As he swung round to stare at her, ignoring the busy traffic, Imogen could see the bemusement in his eyes.

'What?' he protested. 'A runaway bride? I never thought.'

Quickly Imogen gave him her home address, adding tersely, 'And please hurry.'

So far there was no evidence of any pursuit—no sign of either Dracco's sleek Daimler or her stepmother's Rolls-Royce.

* * *

Never had a drive seemed to last so long, nor caused her to sit on the edge of her seat, her fingers clenched into the upholstery in anxiety as she checked constantly to see if they were being followed. But at last the taxi driver was setting her down outside her home, waiting whilst she hurried inside to get the money to pay him—as a bride, there had been no need for her to have any cash with her.

Once she had paid him and soothed his unexpectedly paternal concern for her, she ran back upstairs to her room, dragging off her wedding dress with such force that the fragile fabric ripped. Just as her stepmother and Dracco between them had ripped apart her foolish dreams.

Feverishly she pulled on jeans and a top, hastily emptying the suitcase packed for the honeymoon she and Dracco were to have been taking and refilling it with clothes wrenched blindly off hangers and out of drawers.

She still hadn't really taken in what she had done; all she knew was that she had to get as far away from Dracco as she could and as fast as she could. If, as her stepmother had warned her, he had only been marrying her to gain control of the business then he would not be satisfied until he had that control. She knew how determined he could be. How focused and… A small shudder shook her body. Dracco! Dracco! How could he have done this to her? How could he have humiliated and hurt her so? Tears burning her eyes, Imogen picked up her new cream leather handbag—bought especially for her honeymoon. Inside it was her passport, and the wallet of traveller's cheques Dracco had given her earlier in the week.

'Spending-money,' he had told her with a small smile. The same smile that always made her heart lift and then beat frantically fast, whilst her insides melted and her body longed...

She had counted them after he had gone, her eyes widening as she realised just how much he had given her.

Well, that money would be put to good use now, she reflected bitterly as she allowed herself to enjoy the irony of her using the money Dracco had given her to spend on their honeymoon on funding her escape from him.

She would use it to buy herself a ticket to fly just as far away from him as she could!

'Well, there are seats left on the flight due to leave for Rio de Janeiro in half an hour,' the clerk responded in answer to Imogen's anxious enquiry.

Even whilst she listened to the clerk she couldn't stop herself from glancing nervously over her shoulder, still half expecting to see Dracco's familiar figure bearing down on her, and was chagrined to discover that there was a part of her that was almost desperately hoping that he would be.

But now it was too late. Now she was booked on to the flight for Rio. Shakily she walked over to the check-in desk and handed over her case.

Goodbye, home; goodbye, everything she knew; goodbye, love she had hoped so very very much to have.

Goodbye, Dracco!

CHAPTER ONE

Four years later

THROUGHOUT the flight from Rio Imogen had been rehearsing exactly what she was going to say, and the manner in which she was going to say it. She reminded herself as she did so that she wasn't a naïve girl of just eighteen any more, who knew virtually nothing of the real world or the shadowed, darker side of life, a girl who had been sheltered and protected by her father's love and concern. No; she was a woman now, a woman of twenty-two, who knew exactly what the real world encompassed, exactly how much pain, poverty and degradation it could hold, as well as how much love, compassion and sheer generosity of spirit.

Looking back over the last four years, it seemed almost impossible that she had anything left in common with the girl she had once been. Imogen closed her eyes and lay back in her seat, an economy-class seat, even though she could technically at least have flown home first class. You didn't do things like that when you had spent the last few years working to help destitute orphans who lived in a world where children under five would fight to the death over a scrap of bread. Now, thanks to the small private charitable organisation she worked for, some of those orphans at least were being given a roof over their heads, food, education and, most important of all in Imogen's eyes, love.

Imogen couldn't pin-point exactly when she had first started to regret turning her back on her inheritance—not in any way for her own sake, but for what it could mean to the charity she worked for and the children she so much wanted to help.

Perhaps it had begun when she had stood and watched the happiness light up the face of Sister Maria the day she had announced to them all, in a voice that trembled with thrilled gratitude, that the fund-raising they had all worked so hard on that year had raised a sum of money that was only a tithe of the income Imogen knew she could have expected from her inheritance—never mind its saleable value.

All she did know was that increasingly over recent months she had begun to question the wisdom of what she had done and just how right she was to allow pride to stand in the way of all that she could do to benefit the charity.

And, as if that weren't enough, she had begun, too, to wonder how her friends and fellow workers would view her if they knew how wilfully and indeed selfishly she was refusing to use her own assets where they could do so much good. Pride was all very well but who exactly was paying for her to have the luxury of indulging in it? These and other equally painful questions had been causing Imogen to battle within herself for far too long. And now finally she had come to a decision she felt ashamed to have taken so long in reaching.

The nuns were so kind, so gentle, so humbly grateful for every scrap of help they received. They would never blame or criticise her, Imogen knew, but she was beginning to blame and criticise herself.

During her years in Rio Imogen had learned to protect and value her privacy, to guard herself from any unwanted questions, however kindly meant. Her trust was not something she gave lightly to others any more. Her past was a taboo subject and one she discussed with no one.

She had made friends in Rio, it was true, but her past was something she had kept to herself, and the friends she had made had all been kept at something of a distance—especially the men. Falling in love, being in love—these were things that hurt too much for her to even think about, never mind risk doing. Not after Dracco. *Dracco.* Even now she still sometimes dreamed about him. Dreams that drained her so much emotionally that for days afterwards she ached with pain.

There was no one to whom she wanted to confide just how searing her sense of loss and aloneness had been when she had first arrived in the city, or just how often she had been tempted to change her mind and return home. Only her pride had stopped her—that and the letter she had sent to her father's solicitor a week after her arrival in Rio, informing him that she was disassociating herself completely from her past life. She had said that she wanted nothing to do with the inheritance her father had left her and that henceforward she wanted to be allowed to lead her own life, on her own. She had made her letter as formal as possible, stating that under no circumstances did she want any kind of contact with either her stepmother or Dracco.

She had, of course, omitted to put any address on the

letter, and as an added precaution she had used the last of the money Dracco had given her to fly to America, where she had posted her letter before returning to Rio.

In order to support herself she had found work both as an interpreter and a teacher, and it had been through that work that she had become involved with the sisters and their children's charity.

It had taken her what was now a guilt-inducing amount of time to bring herself to take the action she was now taking, and she still felt acutely ashamed to remember the look of bemused disbelief on Sister Maria's face when she had haltingly explained to her that she was not the penniless young woman she had allowed everyone to believe she was.

Sister Maria's total lack of any attempt to question or criticise her had reinforced Imogen's determination to put matters right as speedily as she could.

Initially she had believed that it would be enough simply for her to write to her father's solicitor, explaining that she had changed her mind about the income she could receive under her father's will. She had explained in the simplest possible terms how she wished to use it to benefit Rio's pitifully needy street children. It had distressed her to receive a letter back not from Henry Fairburn but from an unknown David Bryant. He had introduced himself in the letter as Henry's successor and nephew, explaining that his uncle had died and that he had taken over the business.

As to Imogen's income from the inheritance left to her by her father, the letter had continued, he considered that because of the complications of the situation it would be necessary for her to return to England to put her wishes into action, and he had advised her to lose no time in doing so.

Of course, she had baulked at the idea of returning home. But, after all, what was there really for her to fear other than her own fear?

There was certainly no need for her to fear her long-dead love for Dracco. How could there be?

There had been no contact between them whatsoever, and for all that she knew he and Lisa could now be living together in blissful happiness. They certainly deserved one another. She had never met two people who matched one another so exactly in terms of cold-bloodedness.

It was a great pity that her father had seen fit to make Dracco one of her trustees and an even greater one that Henry, her other trustee, was no longer alive. Imogen wasn't quite sure just what the full legal position with regard to her inheritance and her rights was, but no doubt this David Bryant would be able to advise her on that. And on the other crumple in the otherwise smooth surface of her life that she really ought to get ironed out?

That small and impossible-to-blank-out fact that she and Dracco were still legally, so far as she was aware, married?

Disconcertingly the only gently chiding comment Sister Maria had made when Imogen had been explaining her situation had been a soft reminder that the vows of marriage were supposed to be for life!

Foolishly she had never bothered to get their marriage annulled. She had been far too terrified in those early days that Dracco might somehow persuade her to return home and to their marriage.

Now, of course, she had no such fear, and no need for the status of a single woman either, other than as a salve to her own pride, a final step into a Dracco-free future.

She was also looking forward to, as she had promised she would, writing to Sister Maria to tell her that everything was going smoothly and that she would soon be returning to Rio.

Her stomach muscles tensed with a nervous apprehension that she told herself firmly was entirely natural as the plane began its descent into Heathrow Airport.

The Imogen who had left Heathrow four years earlier had been pretty in a soft, still-girlish way, but the woman she had become could never in a thousand years have been described as wishy-washily pretty. The hardship of a life that was lived without any kind of luxury, a life that was spent giving one hundred and fifty per cent physical commitment and two hundred and fifty per cent emotional love, had stripped Imogen's body of its late-teenage layer of protective flesh and honed her face to a delicately boned translucency. This revealed not just her stunningly perfect features and the deep, intense amethyst of her amazing eyes, but also gave her a luminosity that was almost spiritual and that made people turn to look at her not just once but a second and then a third time.

She was dressed simply in soft chinos and a white cotton shirt, but no woman could possibly live in Rio without absorbing something of the sensuality of its people, of a culture that flagrantly and unselfconsciously worshipped the female form. Brazilian clothes were cut in a way that was unique, and not even the loose fit of what she was wearing could conceal the narrowness of Imogen's waist, the high curve of her breasts, the unexpected length of her legs, but most of all the rounded curve of her bottom.

Her dark hair meant that her skin had adapted well to the South American sun, which had given her a warm, ripe, peachy glow. As she raised her hand to shield her eyes from the shaft of sunlight breaking through the grey cloud the gold watch her father had given her shortly before his death glinted in the light, emphasising the fragility of her wrist. A group of stewardesses walking past her looked enviously at the careless way she had tied the tangled thickness of her curls back off her face with an old white silk scarf.

Taking a deep breath, Imogen summoned a taxi. Once inside it, she studied the piece of paper she had removed from her purse, and gave the address written on it to the driver.

As he repeated it he commented, 'Bute Wharf. That'll be one of them new developments down by the river.'

Imogen smiled dutifully in acknowledgement of his comment but said nothing. She had asked the advice of her solicitor on where to stay, specifying that it had to be reasonably close to his office, and cheap.

To her astonishment, not only had he replied with a terse note that explained that he had made arrangements for her to stay 'at the enclosed address' but which had also enclosed a cheque to cover her air fare. A first-class fare—although she had chosen not to make use of it.

This particular Docklands area of London was unfamiliar to her and Imogen's eyes widened a little as she studied it through the taxi window: streets filled with expensive cars, young men and women dressed in designer clothing, an air about the whole area of affluence and prestige. Was this really the kind of place where she was going to find cheap accommodation? She began to panic a little, wondering if the solicitor had misunderstood her request.

The taxi was pulling up outside an impressive apartment block. Getting out, Imogen glanced up uncertainly at her surroundings, paying off the taxi and then picking up her one small case before squaring her shoulders and heading determinedly towards the entrance.

As she did so she was vaguely aware of the dark shadow of a large car gliding into the space left by the taxi, but she paid no attention to it, too busy making sure that she had the right address to concern herself with it.

Yes, the address was the same one the solicitor had given her.

A little warily Imogen walked into the luxurious atrium that was the apartment block's lobby and then stopped, drawn by some compelling force she couldn't resist to turn round and stare, and then stare again. Her breath froze in shock in her lungs as she recognised the man casually slamming the door of the car she had been so vaguely aware of before turning to stride determinedly through the entrance towards her, exclaiming coolly as he did so, 'Imo! I had hoped to meet you at the airport, but somehow I missed you.'

'Dracco!'

How weak her voice sounded, shaky and thin, the

voice of a child, a girl… Fiercely she tried to clear her throat, reminding herself that she was twenty-two and an adult, but her senses had shut down. They were concentrating exclusively on Dracco.

Four years hadn't changed him as much as she believed they had changed her, but then, he had already been an adult when she had left.

He still possessed that same aura of taut male sexual power she remembered so vividly, only now, as a woman, she was instantly, intensely aware of just how strong it was. It was like suddenly seeing something which had previously only been a hazy image brought sharply into focus, and she almost recoiled physically from the raw reality of it.

Had she forgotten just how magnetically sexy he was or had she simply never known, been too naïve to know? Well, if so, she wasn't now.

His hair was still as dark as she remembered, but cut shorter, giving him a somewhat harder edge. His eyes were harder than she remembered too. Harder and scrutinising her with a coldness that made her shiver.

'You didn't travel first class.'

'You knew that I was coming?' Try as she might, Imogen couldn't keep her appalled shock to herself.

'Of course. I'm your trustee, remember, and since the purpose of your visit is to discuss your inheritance…'

Her trustee! Well, of course she knew that, but somehow she had assumed, believed, that it would be David Bryant she would be talking to and that he would act as a negotiator between herself and Dracco. The last thing she wanted or needed was to be confronted by him like this when she was already feeling nervous and on edge. Not to mention jet-lagged.

Determined to grab back at least some small measure of control, she threw at him acidly, 'I'm surprised that Lisa isn't with you.'

'Lisa?'

She could see from his sharply incisive tone and the look he was giving her that he didn't like her pointed comment.

'This was nothing to do with Lisa,' he told her coldly.

Of course, he would want to protect his lover, Imogen acknowledged angrily.

The shocking realisation of how much she wanted to hurl at him all the accusations she had thought safely disarmed and vanquished years ago hit her nerve-endings like the kick of a mule. The old Imogen might well have given in and done so, but there had been something in the way he had looked at her when he had reminded her that he was her trustee that was warning her to tread very carefully.

Surely it was only a matter of formality for her to be able to reclaim the income she had previously rejected? It was, after all, legally hers, wasn't it?

Surely David Bryant would have told her, warned her, if this wasn't the case or if he had foreseen problems, rather than encouraging her to come all this way?

When it came to disposing of her share of the business, Imogen felt that she was on firmer ground. Since Dracco had been willing to marry her to secure it, surely it made sense that he would be delighted to be given legal control of her share of it in return for guaranteeing its income would be given to the charity?

After all, if she wished she could always sell it on the open market! Knowing that she held that power, that threat over him, helped to rally her courage.

Dracco had reached her now, and Imogen discovered that one thing hadn't changed. She still had to tilt her head right back to look up into his eyes when he stood next to her.

Too late to regret now the comfortable low-heeled pumps she was wearing.

'Come on.' As he spoke Dracco was propelling her forward, the fear of experiencing the sensation of that powerful long-fingered hand of his, placed firmly in the small of her back, causing her to hurry in the direction he was indicating.

What was the matter with her? Why on earth should she fear Dracco touching her now? Once she had feared it because then she had known that even the briefest and most non-sexual contact with him was enough to make her aching body feel as though it might explode with longing, but those days were over! All around her on the streets of Rio she had seen the living, suffering evidence of what happened when two human beings indulged in their sexual desires. She would never abandon her child—never in a million years—but then, she was not a girl, a child herself, penniless and without any means of support. No, that wasn't the point. The point was…the point was…

Dizzily, dangerously Imogen realised that she was having a hard time focusing on anything logical or sensible; that she was, in fact, finding it virtually impossible to concentrate on anything other than Dracco himself.

'It's this way.'

Automatically she followed him towards the glass-walled lift, numbly aware of the brief nod of the hovering uniformed commissionaire as he greeted Dracco with a respectful, 'Good afternoon, Mr Barrington.'

'Afternoon, Bates,' Dracco responded calmly. 'Family OK?'

'Yes, they're fine, and young Robert's over the moon about that job you got for him.'

The smile Dracco gave the doorman suddenly made him look far less formidable and reminded Imogen of the smiles he once used to give her. An almost unbearably tight pain filled her chest, which she firmly put down to the speed with which the lift was surging upwards.

'Still scared of heights? Don't look down,' Dracco told her coolly. 'Heaven knows why, but for some reason every architect in the city seems to have decided that glass-walled lifts are the in thing.'

Where once he would have made such a comment in a voice that was ruefully amused, now he sounded terse and cold. Well, there was no reason why he should show her any warmth, was there?

But why shouldn't he? She had, after all, spared him the trouble of having to pretend that he had wanted to marry her or that he cared about her, and she had given him what he really wanted at the same time. In the letter she had sent to Henry renouncing her inheritance she had given Dracco complete and total authority to use the power that came with her share of the business as he saw fit.

In doing so, she had known beyond any kind of doubt that Dracco would uphold her father's business ideals and aims. In that regard at least she had known she could trust him totally.

She had closed her eyes when the lift started to move, but unexpectedly the images, the memories suddenly tormenting her were even worse in their own way than the heights she feared. She would, she knew, never forgive Dracco for what he had tried to do; for the way he had tried to manipulate her; for the way he had abused the trust her father had placed in him.

The lift shivered to a silent stop.

'You can open your eyes now,' she heard Dracco telling her wryly.

As she edged out of the lift Imogen saw that they had stopped at the floor marked 'Penthouse Suite'.

Penthouse suite. Her solicitor had roomed her in a penthouse suite? Discomfort flickered down her spine. She just knew that this was going to be expensive.

It had taken her a long time to get used to the shared dormitory she had slept in when she had first arrived in Rio, but when she finally found her own small apartment for the first few weeks she had actually missed the presence of the other girls. Now, though, she had to admit to relishing the privacy and the luxury of having her own bathroom.

'I asked David Bryant to find me somewhere cheap and convenient for his office,' she murmured as Dracco produced a key and unlocked the apartment's door.

Imogen could see his eyebrows rise as he listened to her.

'Well, he's complied with both those instructions,' he informed her. 'His office isn't that far away, and you're staying here as my guest.'

'Your guest?'

Imogen froze on the spot, staring at him with wide eyes, whilst Dracco pushed the door to, enclosing them both in the intimacy of the empty hallway.

'Your guest?' Imogen repeated starkly. 'This is your apartment?'

'Yes,' Dracco confirmed. 'When David told me that you'd specified you wanted to stay somewhere close to his office I told him that you might as well stay here with me. After all, there's a great deal we need to discuss...and not just about your inheritance.'

He was, Imogen recognised, looking pointedly at her left hand, the hand from which she had removed the wedding ring he had placed on it, throwing it as far as she could through the open taxi window on her way to Heathrow, too blinded by tears to see where it landed, and too sick at heart to care.

'You mean...' She paused and flicked her tongue tip over her suddenly dry lips, nervously aware of Dracco's iron gaze following her every movement.

'You mean our marriage?' she guessed shakily.

'I mean our marriage,' Dracco confirmed.

'You know,' he told her conversationally as he bent to pick up her lightweight case, 'for a woman who is still a virgin, you look...decidedly unvirginal.'

Imogen tried to convince herself that the rushing sensation of faintness engulfing her was caused by the airlessness of the hallway rather than by what Dracco had said, but still she heard herself demanding huskily, 'How...how do you know?'

'That you are still a virgin?' Dracco completed for

her. 'I know everything there is to know about you, Imo… After all, you are my wife…'

His wife!

Imogen felt sick; filled with a cold, shaky disbelief and an even colder fear. This was not what she had expected; what she had steeled herself to deal with.

During the long flight from Rio she had forced herself to confront the fear that had raised its threatening head in her nightmares in the days leading up to her journey. She had been terrified that somehow, totally against her will and all logic, if she were to see Dracco again she might discover a dangerous residue of her teenage love for him had somehow survived; that it was waiting, ready to explode like a time bomb, to destroy her new life and the peace of mind she had fought so hard for. But now! Now it wasn't love that Dracco was arousing inside her but a furious mixture of anger and hostility.

So she was still a virgin—was that a crime?

'You have no right to pry into my life, to spy on me,' she began furiously, but Dracco refused to allow her to continue.

'We are still married. I am still your husband; you are still my wife,' he pointed out coldly.

Imogen turned away to conceal her expression from him. Married in the eyes of the church, perhaps, but surely not in the eyes of the law, since their marriage had never been consummated. And that certainly didn't give Dracco the right to claim her as his wife in a voice that suggested… Wearily Imogen shook her head. Now she was letting her imagination run away with her. Thinking she had heard possessiveness in Dracco's voice.

His words had given her a shock. Why on earth hadn't Dracco had the marriage set aside? He, after all, loved another woman—her stepmother!

Even after all these years it still filled her with acute nausea and disgust to think of Dracco with Lisa. Her father's wife and the man her father had loved and valued so very much. Had Dracco slept with Lisa whilst her father was still alive? Had they…? Had he…? Unstoppably all the questions she had fiercely forbidden herself to even think before suddenly stormed through her. The images they were conjuring up sickened her, causing a red-hot boiling pain in her middle.

All those years ago, Dracco had implied to her that he was marrying her to protect her, when all he had really wanted to protect had been his own interests!

Tiredly Imogen closed her eyes. She had come to England for one purpose and one purpose only and that was to claim whatever money might be owing to her. And to persuade Dracco to transfer her interest in the business into the name of the charity so that in future it could benefit direct from her inheritance. Anything else…

'I haven't come back to discuss our marriage, Dracco.' Firmly Imogen took a deep breath, determined to take control of the situation. 'I've already written to David Bryant, explaining what I want, and that is—'

'To give away your inheritance to some charity,' Dracco interrupted her grimly. 'No, Imo,' he told her curtly. 'As your trustee, there's no way I would be fulfilling my moral obligation towards you if I agreed, and as your husband…'

She ached to be able to challenge him, to throw caution to the wind and demand furiously to know just when moral obligations had become important to him. But some inner instinct warned her against going too far. This wasn't how their interview was supposed to go. She was an adult now, on an equal footing with Dracco, and not a child whom he could dictate to.

'Legally the money is mine,' she reminded him, having mentally counted to ten and calmed herself down a little.

'Was yours,' Dracco corrected her harshly. 'You insisted that you wanted nothing to do with your inheritance—and you put that insistence in writing—remember.'

Imogen took another deep breath. The situation was proving even more fraught with difficulties than she had expected.

'I did write to Uncle Henry saying that,' she agreed, pausing to ask him quietly, 'When did he die? I had no idea.'

Dracco had turned away from her, and for a moment Imogen thought that he had either not heard her question or that he did not intend to answer it, but then without turning back to her he said coldly, 'He had a heart attack shortly after…on the day of our wedding.'

Horrified, Imogen could only make a soft, anguished sound of distress.

'Apparently he hadn't been feeling well before the ceremony,' Dracco continued as though he hadn't heard her. 'When he collapsed outside the church…' He stopped whilst Imogen battled against her shock. 'I went with him to the hospital. They hoped then… But he had a second attack whilst he was in Intensive Care which proved fatal.'

'Was it...?' Too shocked to guard her thoughts, Imogen blurted out shakily, 'Was it because of me? Because I...?'

'He had been under a tremendous amount of pressure,' Dracco told her without answering her anguished plea for reassurance. 'Your father's death had caused him an immense amount of work, and it seems that there had been certain warning signs of a heart problem which he had ignored. He wasn't a young man—he was ten years older than your father.' He paused and then said abruptly, 'He asked me to tell you how proud he had been to give you away.'

Tears blurred Imogen's eyes. She had a mental image of her father's solicitor on the morning of her wedding, dressed in his morning suit, his silver-grey hair immaculately groomed. In the car on the way to the church he had taken hold of her hand and patted it a little awkwardly. He had been a widower, like her father, with no children of his own, and Imogen had always sensed a certain shyness in his manner towards her. Her father had been a very loving man and she had desperately missed the father-daughter warmth of their relationship. She had known from the look in his eyes that, like her, Henry Fairburn had been thinking about her father on that day.

She had been sad to learn of his death from his nephew, but she had never imagined...

'If you're going to throw yourself into a self-indulgent bout of emotional guilt, I shouldn't bother,' Dracco was warning her hardly. 'His heart attack was a situation waiting to happen and would have happened whether or not you had been there.'

Somehow, instead of comforting and reassuring her, Dracco's blunt words were only making her feel worse, Imogen acknowledged.

'I don't want to argue with you, Dracco,' she said quietly. 'You are a wealthy man in your own right. If you could just see the plight of these children…'

'It is a good cause, yes, involvement with the shelter. My sources inform me that—'

'Your sources?' Imogen checked him angrily. 'You have no right—'

'Surely you didn't think I would allow you to simply disappear without any trace, Imo? For your father's sake, if nothing else; I owed it to him to—'

'I can't believe that even someone like you could stoop so low. To have me watched, spied on,' Imogen breathed bitterly.

'You're overreacting,' Dracco told her laconically. 'Yes, I made enquiries to ascertain where you were and what you were doing and with whom,' he agreed. 'Anyone would have done the same in the circumstances. You were a young, naïve girl of eighteen. Anything could have happened to you.'

He was frowning broodingly and Imogen had to shake herself free of the foolish feeling that he had been genuinely concerned about her.

'It doesn't matter what you say, Dracco, I'm not going to give up,' she warned him determinedly. 'The shelter needs money so desperately, and I warn you now that I'm prepared to do whatever it takes to make sure it gets mine.'

The silence that followed her passionate outburst caused a tiny sliver of apprehension to needle its way into Imogen's nervous system. Dracco was looking at her as though…as though…

Why had she never realised as a girl how very hawkish and predatory he could look, almost demonically so? She shivered and instantly blamed her reaction on the change of continent.

'Well, you're a woman now, Imo, and not a girl and, as you must have surely come to realise, nothing in this life comes without a price. You handed your inheritance over to me of your own accord. Now you wish me to hand it back to you, and not only the income which your share of the business has earned these last four years, but the future income of that share as well.'

'It belongs to me,' Imogen insisted. 'The terms of my father's will stated that it would become mine either on my thirtieth birthday or when I married, whichever happened first.'

'Mmm…' Dracco gave her a look she could not identify.

'You have told me what it is you want me to give you, Imo, but what are you prepared to give me in exchange for my agreement—supposing, of course, that I am prepared to give it?'

Imogen started to frown. What could she give him?

'We are still married,' Dracco was reminding her yet again. 'Our marriage was never annulled.'

Imogen's face cleared. 'You want an annulment,' she guessed, ignoring the sharp, unwanted stab of pain biting into her heart and concentrating instead on clinging determinedly to the relief she wanted to feel. 'Well, of course I will agree, and—'

'No, I do not want an annulment,' Dracco cut across her hurried assent. 'Far from it.'

CHAPTER TWO

'YOU don't want an annulment?' Imogen stared at Dracco as though she couldn't believe what she had heard. 'What...what do you mean?' she demanded.

She could hear the nervous stammer in her voice and despised herself for it. Dracco couldn't mean that he wanted to remain married to her. That was impossible. And just as impossible to accept was that sharp, shocking thrill of excitement his words had given her.

Dracco watched her carefully. As Imogen's trustee, it was his moral duty to safeguard her inheritance for her, to be worthy of the trust her father had placed in him, and that was something he fully intended to do. And if in helping her he was able to progress his own personal agenda, then so much the better! And as for him telling her just why...but, no...that was totally out of the question. Fate had generously dealt some very powerful cards into his hand, and now it was up to him to play them successfully. And he intended to play them and to win!

Imogen felt a nervous tremor run through her body as she waited for Dracco's response. His expression was hard and unreadable, his eyes cold and distant.

'I hope that you don't need me to remind you of just how much your father meant to me,' he began abruptly.

'I know that you married me because of his will,' Imogen responded ambiguously. She had wanted to give Dracco a subtle warning that she was not the naïve girl who had trusted him so implicitly any longer, but even she was shocked by the swiftness with which he decoded her message. Shocked and, if she was honest, just a little bit apprehensive when she saw the immediate and fearsome blaze of anger in the look he gave her.

'And what exactly is that supposed to mean?' Dracco challenged her softly.

Imogen took a deep breath. There was no way she was going to allow him to face her down! There was too much at stake. She had a responsibility to those who were dependent on her for her help.

'I was very young when I married you, Dracco,' she told him as calmly as she could. 'My father's will, as we both know, stipulated that I should have control of my share of the business upon my marriage. Naturally, since I was so young, I would have deferred to you where matters of business were concerned, so that in effect you would have had full control of the business—and the income it generated. Of course, had you chosen to sell the business and utilise the profits from that sale on your own behalf…'

'What?'

For a moment Dracco looked almost as though she had shocked him.

'If you are trying to imply that I married you for financial gain then let me tell you you're way off the mark. In fact, I am wealthier now than your father ever was—thanks, I have to admit, to everything he taught me.'

He was speaking to her as though he were admonishing a child, Imogen decided angrily.

'So why exactly did you marry me, then?' she asked him sharply.

'You know why.' He started to turn away from her so that she couldn't see his face, his voice becoming curt.

Imogen could sense that her question had made him uneasy in some way. Because he felt guilty? Well he might!

'Yes, I do, don't I?' Imogen agreed acerbically. 'My father—'

'Your father was a man I admired more than any other man I have ever met.' Dracco cut across what she had been about to say, his tone warning her against questioning the truth of his words. 'In fact, in the early years of our friendship, I often wished that he had been *my* father. I have never met a man I have respected or loved as much as I did John Atkins, Imogen. I felt proud to have his friendship and his trust. He was everything I myself most wanted to be. He was everything that my own father was not.'

He paused, whilst Imogen silently swallowed the huge lump of emotion in her throat.

Dracco's father had left his mother whilst Dracco had still been a baby; a gambler and a womaniser, he had been killed in a drunken brawl when Dracco had been in his early teens.

'I have never lost either my admiration or my love for your father, Imo, nor the wish that he and I might share a closer, more personal tie.' He paused meaningfully whilst Imogen fidgeted with anxiety. Whatever conditions Dracco imposed on his agreement to hand over her inheritance, Imogen knew that somehow she would have to meet them. There was no way she wanted to disappoint the nuns now, nor did she intend to do anything that would prevent her being able to improve the lot of those who were dependent on the shelter.

'Your father could never be my father, Imo, but he could be the grandfather of my son—our son,' Dracco told her meaningfully.

His son…their son. Stupefied, Imogen gaped at him. She couldn't possibly have heard him correctly.

'No!' she protested frantically. 'You can't mean it.' But she could see from his expression that he did, and her heart somersaulted inside her ribcage and then banged dizzyingly against her ribs themselves.

'No,' she whispered painfully. 'I can't. I won't! This is blackmail, Dracco,' she accused him. 'If you want a child so much—'

'I don't want "a" child, Imo,' he cut across her coolly. 'Haven't you been listening to what I said? What I want is your father's grandchild. My blood linked to his, and only you can provide me with that.'

'You're mad,' Imogen gasped. 'This is like something out of the Dark Ages…it's…I won't do it!' she told him fiercely.

'Then I won't give you your money,' Dracco informed her in a voice that was dangerously soft.

'You'll have to… I'll take you to court. I'll…' Imogen began wildly, but once again Dracco stopped her, shaking his head as he told her unkindly,

'Somehow I don't think a court would agree to you giving away your birthright. Especially if it was to be implied that part of the reason your father set up his will as he did was because he feared that you were not financially astute enough to protect your own interests.'

Imogen glared furiously at him. 'You wouldn't dare,' she began, but Dracco was smiling at her, a mocking smile that didn't touch his eyes as he told her softly, 'Try me!'

Imogen shook her head in angry disbelief. This was emotional manipulation at its worst. How on earth could she ever have loved Dracco? Right now she positively hated him.

'You can't do this,' she protested, her face raw with emotion as she told him shakily, 'If you could see these children—they have nothing, Dracco. Less than nothing. They need help so badly!'

'And they can have it, Imo,' Dracco told her calmly, 'but not from your inheritance. As your trustee, I cannot allow that, but—' he paused and looked at her, his penetrating gaze holding her own and refusing to let her look away '—but,' he repeated coolly, 'as your husband,' Dracco continued with a pseudo-gentleness that made her tense her stomach muscles against whatever it was he was going to say, 'as your husband,' he stressed with deliberate emphasis, 'I would be quite prepared to promise to pay one million pounds to the shelter now, and another one million when you give birth to our child.'

If Imogen hadn't already decided she hated Dracco she knew she would have done so now. How could he be so cynical, so cruel, so corrupt? Two million pounds! He must be rich indeed if he could afford to part with so much money so easily and just so that... He had loved and revered her father, she knew that, and she could even see too why he might want to have a child who carried her father's blood. But to go about it in such a way, when he knew that he would be forcing her to have sex with him and when he knew too that he didn't love her… Imogen couldn't stop herself from shuddering with angry loathing.

'I…I need time to think,' she told him defiantly.

'To think, or to run away again? I thought this charity was all-important to you, Imo, but it seems…'

'Stop it.' Covering her ears with her hands, Imogen turned away from him.

His cruelty appalled her but she couldn't stop herself from acknowledging the truth of what he was saying. When she thought about the difference his money would make to Rio's homeless street children Imogen knew that she could not possibly put her own needs before theirs.

'So do we have a deal—two million for your charity, a wife and, hopefully, your father's grandchild for me?'

Somehow Imogen managed not to show how desperately tempted she was to refuse. Summoning all her courage, she took a deep breath and agreed huskily, 'Yes.'

Bleakly Imogen stared out of the window of Dracco's car—a sleek silver BMW now and not the Daimler she remembered him driving—as they sped through the uniquely green English countryside. She had not asked Dracco where they were going, had not addressed any questions or conversation to him at all, in fact, since she had woken up in his city apartment earlier on in the day. His apartment but thankfully not his bed; no, she had been spared that at least for now, having slept alone in his guest room.

She had no idea where they were going and had no intention of asking. All Dracco had told her once he had ascertained that she was prepared to accede to the terms he had proposed to her—an agreement she had thrown at him with flashing eyes and an angrily set mouth as she tried to remind herself that his proposition surely demeaned him far more than it demeaned her—was that he was taking her to the house that was going to be her home.

'Stop behaving like a tragedy queen, Imo,' she heard him saying drily to her. 'It doesn't suit you and, besides, there's no need.'

'No need? After what you've done,' Imogen exploded.

'After what I've done?' Dracco checked her. 'I haven't done anything other than offer you a deal.'

'A deal!' Indignation flashed from Imogen's eyes. 'You're blackmailing me into having a child with you.' Quickly she turned away from him before he could sense the emotions she was struggling to overcome. 'What's going to happen once you have your child, Dracco?'

'What do you think is going to happen?' he challenged her sharply. 'No child of mine is going to be abandoned by either of its parents, Imogen.'

'You expect me to stay married to you?'

Surely that wasn't actually relief she could feel spreading through her tensed muscles?

'What I expect is that you and I will stay married to one another for just as long as our child needs us to be.

What were you expecting?' he demanded as he skilfully negotiated a tight bend.

Imogen shook her head, not wanting him to see how relieved she was that he wasn't going to try to separate her from her child, to send her away whilst he brought it up alone. Because she knew that, no matter what she might think about Dracco himself, no matter how much she might loathe and hate him for what he was doing, she would never be able to walk away from her baby.

She frowned as she suddenly recognised the countryside they were driving through, her heart starting to beat increasingly heavily as the road dropped down into the village where she had grown up. At the end of the village street Dracco turned left. The lane started to climb steeply and, even though it had been four years since she had last travelled down it, Imogen remembered every inch of it. It had been down this road that Dracco had driven her to school; down this road that he had driven her when he had come to fetch her the day her father had died; down this road she had travelled on her way to her wedding.

'You've bought our old house.' She said it as a statement rather than a question, her voice flat as she fought to control her emotions.

'I was already negotiating for it before our wedding,' Dracco answered her unemotionally. 'It was supposed to be a surprise wedding present for you. I knew how much you hated the idea of Lisa selling it. By the time it became obvious that you weren't going to be around to collect any wedding presents from me or anyone else, it was too late to pull out of the deal.' He gave a small dismissive shrug. 'I suppose I could have put it back on the market, but…'

Dracco had turned into the house's familiar drive and for a moment, as the car crunched over the gravel and came to a halt outside the front door, Imogen almost felt that if she closed her eyes and then opened them again she would see her father come hurrying towards her.

But her father was dead, and something inside her had died now as well.

'It still looks just the same,' she told Dracco distantly as they both got out of the car. He was a stranger to her, a man she loathed, and yet tonight he would…

Whilst she fought to control the shudders of fear that rocked her Dracco was unlocking the front door.

'Well, you'll find there have been some changes,' he warned her casually. 'I left your father's room as it was, but…' He paused and turned away from her, his voice suddenly shadowed and edged with an emotion she couldn't analyse. 'I haven't really used the house much myself. However, I have made some changes to some of the other rooms.'

When she looked questioningly at him he turned to face her fully and told her bluntly, 'I didn't think that either of us would want to use the rooms that had been your parents', so I had a new master-bedroom suite built on—and the conservatory your father once told me your mother had always wanted. He didn't have the heart to add it after her death, but I thought…' He stopped, his mouth compressing, pushing open the front door without enlightening her as to what his thoughts had been.

Imogen discovered that she was shaking as she followed him inside. It had been down these stairs that she had semi-stumbled on the way to her wedding, her whole world destroyed by Lisa's cruelty, and down them too that she had run in her haste to escape from Dracco and her marriage to him.

Her tastes had changed and matured in the last few years, and she recognised with a sharp pang of pain just how old-fashioned and, yes, shabby the dark red stair carpet her mother had chosen looked. She could almost feel how unloved and desolate the whole house was. Dust motes danced in the sunshine and she could see a film of it lying on the table beneath the ornate Venetian wall mirror that her parents had bought on their honeymoon.

Her mother had been a wonderful homemaker before her illness had struck her down and suddenly Imogen discovered that her own inner eye was itching to bring the house back to life, to turn it back to the love-filled home she could remember. Irritated by her own vulnerability, she demanded sharply of Dracco, 'Why exactly have you brought me here? Apart from the obvious reason, of course.' She added acerbically, 'I have to admit that I'm surprised you don't actually want to conceive this child in my father's bed.'

She stopped in mid-sentence, shocked into silence by the look in his eyes. It was far more dangerous than any verbal warning could have been.

'I have brought you here because this will be your home from now on,' Dracco told her levelly, once he had forced her to drop her gaze from his.

'But you don't live here?' Imogen guessed, thinking about the dust she had seen.

'I haven't been doing,' Dracco agreed. 'There wasn't

any point. But now… A city apartment isn't, in my opinion, the right place to bring up a child.'

'But you will still be spending some time in the city?' Imogen pressed him. Please God, let him say that he would; let him say too that his visits here to the house, to her, and to the bed he was forcing her to share with him, would be infrequent and of short duration.

But instead of answering her directly he surprised her by asking softly, 'What exactly is it about sex that you find so threatening, Imo?'

'Nothing! I don't,' she denied quickly, knowing that her face was burning hotly with a self-consciousness that he had to have seen before she turned defensively away from him. 'It isn't the sex,' she denied doggedly, 'it's you…and the way…'

'I don't believe you,' Dracco told her. 'For a woman of your age still to be a virgin suggests…'

'Suggests what?' Imogen immediately challenged him. 'That I'm choosy about who I give my…' My love, she had been about to say, but she quickly corrected herself and said instead, 'Myself to.'

'Suggests that you're afraid of something,' Dracco continued smoothly, as though she hadn't interrupted him. 'Are you, Imo? Are you afraid?'

'No,' she denied vehemently. But she knew that she was lying. She was afraid. She was very afraid. To her the physical act of sex was inextricably linked with the emotion of love, and she was desperately, mortally afraid that…

That what? That being forced to have sex with Dracco to produce the child he wanted would somehow force her to love him again? How could it?

Last night, lying awake in Dracco's guest room, she had told herself that what she was sacrificing was nothing weighed against what the charity would be gaining and that she was too old to have any right to start feeling sorry for herself. But no amount of trying to be logical about what had happened had helped to ease the sharp, stark pain in her heart—or the fear that accompanied it.

As she moved away from Dracco and walked down the hallway, instinctively heading for her father's study, she could hear him saying wryly, 'A team of cleaners from the village comes in once a month to go over the whole place and I asked them to stock up the fridge and freezer. If their shopping is of the same calibre as their cleaning it might be as well to check the fridge. I have booked a table for dinner at Emporio's for tonight. I trust you do still like Italian food?'

'You're taking me out for dinner?' Imogen couldn't keep the cynicism out of her voice. 'Why not just take me straight to bed? Why waste time—and money? After all, you've already committed yourself to paying two million for it.'

'Stop that at once.'

Imogen gasped as Dracco crossed the distance that separated them with startling speed, taking hold of her forearms, his lean fingers biting hard into her vulnerable flesh as he gave her a small shake.

'You're my wife, Imogen, not some paid harlot. And if I choose to woo you—'

'Woo me!' Imogen could feel the hysterical laughter bubbling up inside her. 'Why on earth would you want to do that?' she challenged him acidly. 'All you really want is a child, my father's grandchild! You can achieve that without going to the expense of buying me dinner. After all, you don't care whether I'm willing or not!'

Dracco released her so quickly that Imogen felt the unwanted shock of his withdrawal from her right through her body. The shaming knowledge that a tiny part of her was actually daring to miss the warm male touch of Dracco's hands on her arms infuriated and frightened her. She told herself that it was just her memory playing tricks, reminding her of a time when she had welcomed and wanted his touch. Welcomed and wanted it! Craved it, ached for it, hungered for it and for him—that was a far more accurate description. Abruptly Imogen dragged her mind back to the present, wincing a little as she saw the furious look Dracco was giving her.

He shook his head, his mouth compressing. 'What I want, and what I intend for this child—*our* child—is that it is born if not out of mutual love then at least out of mutual pleasure.'

His words shocked her, almost thrilled her in some atavistic and explosively dangerous way.

Recklessly Imogen flung back her head and demanded, 'And how is that going to happen when there is no way I could ever want you?'

She could almost hear the seconds ticking by as Dracco looked at her. What could he see…what was he looking for? Her tongue snaked out and touched her suddenly dry lips. Dracco's diamond-hard gaze fastened on her small betraying gesture, seizing on it even more fiercely than his hands had grasped her only minutes earlier. Imogen could almost feel the physical effect of his gaze on her; on her mouth; her body; her senses!

'There is nothing you could ever do that could make

me want you, Dracco. Do you hear me?' The excited fury in her own reiteration frightened her but she refused to allow herself to acknowledge either her fear or her folly.

'Are you challenging me, Imogen?' Dracco asked her softly. 'Because if you want me to prove you wrong I can promise you that I am more than willing to do so. Very much more than willing,' he emphasised with meaningful deliberation.

Imogen's heightened senses relayed to her every aspect of what was happening: the scent of the dust in the air, the limpid warmth of the sun streaming in through the window, which in no way could match the white heat of the fury she could see burning in Dracco's eyes. She shivered, but not with cold, as feelings she had thought long dead sprang to life inside her.

'No!' she whispered painfully beneath her breath. No! It was over. Dead, done... She did not love Dracco any more and she wasn't going to allow herself to do so ever again.

Drawing a shaky breath, she met the look he was giving her.

'You couldn't,' she denied, making herself believe it.

'No? Watch me!' Dracco breathed. 'Just watch me, Imogen. And when you're lying in my bed, my arms, beneath my body, crying out for my possession, wanting me, I shall remind you of this moment.'

CHAPTER THREE

IMOGEN turned away from the window of her childhood bedroom and glanced at her watch.

Seven-thirty; soon she would have to go downstairs and join Dracco, who had warned her that unless she was ready to go out for dinner with him by eight o'clock he would personally 'escort' her downstairs.

'Why are you doing this?' she had demanded in furious frustration.

'Why are you?' he had countered with a coolness that had made her grind her teeth in impotent rage.

'You know why I'm doing it. I don't have any choice.'

'Of course you do,' he had returned promptly. 'You could choose to simply walk away if you wished to do so.'

'The shelter needs money—you know that,' Imogen had argued bitterly.

That was true, and what was also true was that she didn't think she could live with herself if she didn't do everything she could to help. Perhaps a part of her determination to do so had its roots in the fact that she felt guilty because she had withheld her financial help for so long, she acknowledged. But it had taken her a long time to stop being afraid of the power the past had over her; to stop being afraid of the love she had had for Dracco. Now she had overcome that fear!

But to allow Dracco to consummate their marriage; to have his child! Unwillingly Imogen's gaze was drawn back to her bedroom window. Did she really have the resolve, the courage to do that?

It had been from this window that she had watched so many times for her father to come home. She had knelt on the window seat, her elbows on the sill propping up her head as she strained her ears and her eyes for the familiar sound and sight of her father's car. The moment she could hear it she had dashed downstairs, ready to fling herself into his arms just as soon as she could.

Even during the dark days of her mother's final illness her father had never failed to give her the loving reassurance of his time and attention.

And then had come the darker days of his marriage to Lisa, when it had so often been Dracco she had turned to for comfort. Dracco she had waited impatiently to see arriving at the house from the sanctuary of her bedroom.

Her father had loved this house. He had once told her that to him it epitomised everything that a family home should be.

'One day you will bring your children here to see me, Imo,' he had often told her as she grew up.

He had been looking forward to becoming a grandfather.

The scene in front of Imogen's eyes began to blur.

A child. A child that was both a part of him and of herself and Dracco. Her father would have loved that so much, cherished that child so much.

A child. Dracco's child. How often had she sat at this very window and fantasised about that happening; about

Dracco loving her; about that love resulting in the birth of their baby?

Dracco loving her! Angrily Imogen shook away her threatening emotional tears. Dracco did not love her. He simply wanted to share a blood tie with her father. He had told her so.

And yet as she turned away from the bedroom window she could still see so vividly in her mind's eye the three of them walking together up the drive, Dracco, herself and, between them, the dark-haired green-eyed boy-child who shared his father's strong bone-structure and his grandfather's loving smile.

'I must be mad,' Imogen whispered reprovingly to herself as she snatched up her jacket and her bag and headed for her bedroom door.

There was no way she could ever willingly do what Dracco was forcing on her. And surely no way either that she could ever deny that fierce tug of maternal love she had felt so very sharply for the child her own treacherous imagination had conjured up.

When she opened her door she saw Dracco advancing along the landing towards her.

Unlike her, he had changed his clothes, removing the city suit he had been wearing and putting on in its place a more casual pair of cotton chinos and a short-sleeved shirt.

England must have been having a good summer, Imogen acknowledged absently as her gaze slid helplessly along the length of Dracco's bare bronzed arms. There had always been something about his arms that fascinated her, something that had sent a shower of excited girlish sensuality shivering over her skin. In those days, just the thought of Dracco's arms closing round her, holding her in the tender and protective embrace which had been all her innocent mind had then been able to conjure up, had been enough to set off that hot, aching, melting feeling in the pit of her stomach.

Later, as she grew older, it hadn't been so much Dracco's arms holding her she had fantasised about as his hands, touching her, caressing her, stroking and arousing her willing flesh with the kind of intimate and wildly dangerous touch that even in the privacy of her own bed had made her face burn with hot, guilty, excited desire.

He had, Imogen guessed, not only changed his clothes but showered as well, which made her feel uncomfortably aware of the fact that she was still wearing the clothes she had flown into Heathrow in. She had refused to allow herself to change out of a stubborn determination to show him just how unimportant either his opinion of her or his company was. Right now, however, it wasn't a sense of satisfaction in her own stubbornness she was experiencing but rather a very unwanted feeling of gritty discomfort, and general grubbiness, which caused her to reach up defensively to rake her fingers through her tangled curls.

'Too busy to have time to get changed? Never mind, I'm sure Luigi will understand,' Dracco commented.

'You've told Luigi that you…we're…'

'I've told him that you're going to be my dinner guest, yes,' Dracco confirmed. 'I just hope you still like pear and almond tart and honey ice cream.'

Ignoring his dry reference to her teenage love of her

favourite local Italian restaurant's pudding, Imogen demanded wildly, 'What else have you told him?'

Dracco gave a small shrug. 'Nothing,' he denied.

As she absorbed his response Imogen struggled to understand why instead of feeling relief that Dracco hadn't made any kind of public statement about their marriage what she actually felt was a kind of anger.

'But you are going to have to say something?' she persisted. 'We can't just suddenly start living together as a married couple.'

Dracco gave another dismissive shrug. 'As to that, I shall tell people what they will want to hear.'

'Which is?' Imogen challenged him.

'Which is that there has been a rapprochement between us, a mutual agreement with the benefit of hindsight and maturity that we wish to give our marriage a second chance.'

'A second chance?' Imogen couldn't help querying, and then wished that she had not when she saw the look Dracco was giving her.

'Most of them will assume, no doubt, that we were lovers before our marriage, and somehow I doubt that you will want people to know that you are still a virgin.'

Imogen could feel her face reddening.

'Don't flatter yourself that my virginity has anything to do with you!' She threw the words recklessly at him, unaware of just how they might be interpreted or what they might reveal. 'The fact that I haven't...that I'm... Well, that's my business and has nothing to do with anyone else.'

Dracco was already heading for the stairs and automatically Imogen walked with him.

'Just a minute,' he demanded as they reached the hallway.

Warily, Imogen waited as he reached into his pocket and withdrew a small box.

'You're going to need this,' he told her coolly. 'I notice that you aren't wearing the original. This one doesn't have the benefit of a clerical blessing, and I had to guess at the size. You're more slender than you were…'

Without giving her the opportunity to take the box from him, he flipped open the lid, revealing a gold wedding band so similar to the first one he had given her that Imogen had to suppress a superstitious feeling that it was the same ring.

And with it was something she had desperately wished she had not had to leave behind when she had run away—the engagement ring she had not been wearing on the day of her marriage that Dracco had had made for her. It incorporated in an elegant modern setting the three diamonds that had originally been in her mother's engagement ring. Those stones meant so much to her that now as she stared at it, tears stung Imogen's eyes.

'My ring,' she whispered.

'It might be a little bit too big now,' Dracco warned her as she reached for it. He forestalled her and took hold of her hand.

Imogen could feel herself starting to tremble. Against her will she went back in time; she was in church, waiting for Dracco to place his ring on her finger.

Now, as he slid the cold metal over her knuckle, she could remember exactly how she had felt, how much she had wanted to believe that their marriage was more to him than simply a business arrangement.

He was right—the engagement ring was slightly loose, she reflected shakily as he placed it on her finger. Suddenly she was finding it extraordinarily difficult to breathe properly. Her chest felt tightly constricted, her heart was hammering ferociously against her ribs. As though it was happening in slow motion, she was aware of Dracco watching her, waiting, and then lifting her hand towards his mouth.

'No.'

Imogen pulled frantically away from him as the denial was torn from her tense throat. In church he had kissed her hand, the warmth of his lips brushing her cold fingers, making her tremble violently, her whole body ablaze with the intensity of her longing for him as her lover. Yet despite that feeling she had not been able to stop herself from asking him the question that had destroyed her foolish illusions. What would have happened if she had said nothing? But no, she must not even think of asking herself that. Would she really have wanted to live in ignorance of the truth? No, of course she wouldn't!

Unable to bring herself to look at Dracco, she hurried towards the front door. The warm evening sun dazzled her for a moment as they walked outside. She could smell the scent of the roses from the rose bed close to the front door. They had been her mother's favourite flowers and for a moment a wave of nostalgia and pain pierced her. This house held so many memories, so much of her past. The thought of her own child growing up here was unbearably poignant.

Locked into her thoughts, she stood stiffly, staring unseeingly into the distance. The future, with all the hideous complications and emotional pain it now threatened, lay darkly ahead of her. Marriage in these modern times was not necessarily for life, but a child, the bond between parent and child, mother and child, that most certainly was. For her, at least.

'If you're having second thoughts, I shouldn't,' she heard Dracco telling her caustically.

Imogen frowned as the sound of Dracco's voice pierced the bubble surrounding her. For a moment it had almost seemed as though Dracco was actually afraid that she *might* change her mind. He must want this child very badly. Was that the reason he and Lisa had not married, because he had not wanted his child to be her child? Imogen didn't like herself very much for the sharp thrill of pleasure the thought gave her.

'Ah, but you have not changed at all; you are even more beautiful, even more *bella*, than ever!' Luigi was telling Imogen in a voice vibrant with emotion as he showed them to their table.

'If she has not changed then how can she be more *bella*, Luigi? Dracco was demanding drily.

'Then she was a beautiful girl,' Luigi responded with aplomb. 'Now...' His dark eyes glowed with appreciation and approval as he surveyed Imogen in the kind of way that only an Italian male could get away with. 'Now she is a beautiful woman! And what a woman! *Mamma mia!* Ah, but you are one lucky man, my friend, to have such a beautiful wife.'

So Luigi had remembered that they were married!

'Well, it is just as well that one of us can remember what she looked like after one of your lessons in how to eat spaghetti.' Dracco grinned, the dryness of his voice so at odds with the genuine amusement in his eyes that Imogen found somehow she was unable to drag her own gaze away from his face. A face that suddenly, dangerously, looked so much like the face she remembered from her teens, his eyes warm and teasing, his mouth curved into that sizzlingly sexy smile that had made her toes curl up in delight. Luigi's had always been her favourite restaurant, a place she had associated with the happy times in her life.

'I have saved you a special table.' Luigi was beaming as he led them through the busy restaurant to the table that had always been her father's favourite.

A huge lump rose in Imogen's throat. Impulsively she threw her arms around Luigi's rotund frame and gave him a swift hug.

Luigi was hugging her back enthusiastically, then he let her go with unexpected suddenness, stepping back from her whilst apologising to Dracco.

Frowning, Imogen looked from Dracco's now set face to Luigi's apologetic one, unable to fathom out quite what was happening.

'I was forgetting for a moment that you are no longer a little girl but a married woman,' Luigi told her, but it was Dracco he was looking at as he spoke.

As they sat down and Luigi hurried off to get them menus Dracco told her quietly, 'I would prefer it if you didn't flirt with other men.'

'Flirt.' Imogen repeated in disbelief. 'I wasn't flirting. I was just…' She stopped. Why was she bothering to defend herself? She had done nothing wrong. All she had done was to hug Luigi, and for Dracco to accuse her of flirting was totally ridiculous!

'You may still be a virgin, Imo,' Dracco told her, leaning across the table so that no one else could hear what he was saying, 'but that does not make you totally naïve. You're a married woman...my wife.'

'I can't believe I'm hearing this,' Imogen cut in stormily. 'I was just hugging Luigi, that's all. It was nothing at all.'

'It may be nothing to you,' Dracco stopped her grimly. 'But it's a hell of a lot more than I've ever had from you.'

'You're different,' Imogen returned smartly, and then wished she hadn't as she saw his expression. Her stomach writhed nervously.

'Yes. I am different,' Dracco agreed. 'I'm your husband.' He broke off as a young waiter brought them their menus, waiting until he had gone before telling her coldly, 'Before tomorrow night I expect you to move your things into the master bedroom.'

Imogen wondered if he knew just what effect his words had had on her, how shocked and, yes, terrified they had made her. In an effort to conceal those feelings she picked up her menu and, hiding behind it, told him flippantly, 'So much for the threatened seduction.'

When there was no immediate response she carefully lowered her menu, reflecting gleefully that she had at least scored one hit against that impenetrable, tough armour that had both repelled and attracted her for as long as she had known him. But then she saw his face, and the hand holding her menu shook betrayingly.

'Oh, that wasn't a threat, Imo. It was a promise. A promise that I shall do such things to you and for you as to make you scream my name with longing in the darkness of the night; make you ache with your need for my possession; make you—'

'No!'

The denial was strangled in Imogen's throat as the young waiter suddenly appeared and nervously asked if they were ready to order. She knew that her face was burning scarlet with colour, her thoughts a wild, chaotic stampede of disbelief and fury.

How could Dracco say such things to her one minute and the next be calmly discussing with their waiter what exactly the 'specials' were, and whether or not they had a particular wine he wanted?

'You will like this wine, Imo,' he told her calmly once they were alone. 'Your father introduced me to it. It was produced in the same year as you. And, like you...' he continued, his voice dropping to a slow, sensual rasp that licked against Imogen's raw nerve endings in the same way her tormented, traitorous imagination was telling her that his tongue might rasp against the intimate sensitivity of her skin. 'But no!' he told her softly. 'I shall not tell you now what characteristics it shares with you!'

Imogen had ordered mussels as her first course, and her mouth watered when they arrived, cooked in Luigi's special sauce. They had eaten simply and cheaply in Rio, and she was unaware of the way Dracco was watching her as she ate her food with almost childlike enjoyment.

He wondered how she would react if she knew what he was really thinking; feeling; wanting! He took a deep swallow of his wine; like Imogen herself, it had an allure that drew one back almost compulsively to it. His mouth twisted bitterly. It was probably just as well that she didn't know just what was going on inside his head, or inside his body. If she did she would probably run a mile, or rather six thousand miles or so, back to Rio.

Dracco's eyes grew bleak when they rested on Imogen's downbent head as she mopped up the last of her sauce with a piece of bread. If she hadn't come back of her own accord he had had plans in hand for bringing her home. And now that she was home it was up to him to make sure that she stayed there.

As Imogen lifted her head, as if somehow conscious that he was watching her, Dracco dropped his. Observing Dracco's hooded gaze fixed on his plate, Imogen frowned, wondering why on earth she had thought he was looking at her.

'Good; you enjoy that?' Luigi was demanding, beaming as he removed her empty plate.

'Scrumptious,' Imogen assured him, reverting to her favourite childhood word as she started to smile at him and then stopped, the smile which had begun to dimple her mouth fading as she glanced warily at Dracco. Was a married woman allowed to smile at another man? And why should she care anyway whether Dracco approved of her behaviour or not? She didn't, and there was certainly no way she was ever going to allow him to dictate to her what she did!

'Dracco, and Imogen, isn't it? I thought I recognised you. My goodness, what a surprise!'

The angry turbulence of Imogen's thoughts came to

an abrupt halt as she stared into the familiar face of one of her stepmother's closest friends.

Her stepmother and Miranda Walker had been tennis partners and had both had membership at an exclusive local health club. Imogen had liked Miranda only marginally less than she had liked her stepmother. Miranda's husband, she remembered, had spent a lot of time working abroad, but he was obviously back at home now.

It was a shock to see someone so closely and so unpleasantly connected with the past so soon after her return, although she admitted she should perhaps have expected it, as Emporio's had always been the town's most favoured restaurant.

She could almost feel the speculation emanating from Miranda as she continued to stand at their table, ignoring her husband's obvious desire to move away.

'Are we to take it that the two of you are back together?' Miranda was asking with a suggestive coyness that nauseated Imogen. 'I always did think it was rather impetuous of you to run away from him like that, darling.' She laughed as she gave Imogen a fake smile accompanied by a sharply assessing look. 'Wait until I see Lisa. Fancy her not telling me.'

When neither Imogen nor Dracco said anything Miranda demanded excitedly, 'She doesn't know, does she?' There was a pause. 'Oh, dear! She isn't going to be very pleased. She's still in the Caribbean and won't be back for another week yet, will she?' She directed this question at Dracco.

'Excuse me.' Without waiting to hear what Dracco's response was, Imogen got up and headed for the ladies' cloakroom.

It was stupid of her to feel shocked, and as for that daunting, aching pain that was draining her, well, there was no way that could be betrayal. She already knew what the score was; knew how cynically determined Dracco could be to have his cake and eat it.

As she reached the sanctuary of the rest room, and started to run restoring cool water over her wrists, she told herself that she didn't care what his relationship with Lisa was any more. After all, there was only one reason she was here with him tonight and it had nothing to do with any personal desire to be with him. It was because of the children, the shelter, that was all! Just as he was here with her not because he wanted her, but because he wanted her child.

She ought, she told herself judicially, to feel sorry for Lisa.

So far as Imogen was concerned, the whole tone of Miranda's conversation had given away the relationship between Dracco and her stepmother. Had he told Lisa what he was planning to do? Somehow Imogen rather suspected that he had not.

Carefully drying her hands, she took a deep breath. It was time for her to go back.

There was no sign of Miranda or her husband when Imogen returned to the table. Without saying anything, she sat down. Her head had started to ache badly. She felt almost as though she was about to come down with a bad case of flu; her throat felt tight and sore, she felt slightly sick, and—

Imogen gave a small gasp as the whole room spun round.

'Imogen. Are you all right?'

Somehow Dracco was standing next to her.

'No,' she told him muzzily. 'I feel sick.'

Frowning, Dracco glanced from Imogen's barely touched glass of wine to her white face.

'Let's get you outside. You might feel better in the fresh air.'

As Imogen felt him moving closer to her she instinctively shrank away from him. Listening to Miranda had underlined for her all the most unpalatable aspects of her situation that she least wanted to think about. The hands that Dracco was reaching out to her had touched Lisa, her enemy; the voice expressing distant concern for her had no doubt whispered soft, passionate words of desire and wanting to her stepmother. The act of procreation he would share with her would be a cold, mechanical, loveless thing, very different from his physical intimacy with Lisa... Imogen shuddered, unable to control her revulsion. No wonder she felt so sick.

Imogen saw in Dracco's eyes his reaction to her instinctive rejection of him. Bending his head, he muttered angrily to her, 'We're supposed to be giving our marriage a second chance. Remember?'

'You don't want to give our marriage a second chance,' Imogen managed to hiss swiftly. 'You just want...'

Somehow Dracco had shepherded her to the door, and was opening it. Greedily Imogen gulped in the fresh evening air. Her dizziness was beginning to clear, her nausea retreating.

'Want to tell me what all that was about?'

Warily she looked at Dracco. 'I felt sick, that's all. Surely it's hardly surprising in the circumstances.

Nothing's changed, has it, Dracco?' she challenged him bitterly.

'Did you expect it to have done? Don't you think that's rather naïve?'

The hard expression she could see in his eyes made her muscles clench. He wasn't even remotely ashamed of what he was doing.

'You didn't tell me that Lisa was still living locally,' she told him bitterly. He was shrugging dismissively as though he found her anger an irrelevance, and his attitude goaded her into a fiercely hostile reaction.

'Lisa was married to my father. She's—'

He interrupted her. 'I know what Lisa is, Imo.'

'You know but you don't care, do you?' Imogen couldn't stop herself from saying the words, even though she could already see the truth in his eyes.

Just as she could hear the anguish shaking through her own voice.

She heard Dracco mutter something under his breath before telling her grimly, 'You always were too damned sensitive for your own good. And too damned…' Whatever he had been about to say was lost as the restaurant door opened and another couple emerged, pausing to give them a briefly curious look, no doubt able to sense the hostility and tension crackling between them. Taking hold of Imogen's arm, Dracco informed her curtly, 'This isn't the place for a discussion of this nature,' as he propelled her to where he had parked his car.

'Let go of me,' Imogen demanded through gritted teeth as they reached it. 'I can't bear to have you touching me, Dracco. Not now. Not after…' She stopped as she saw the intensity of the fury darkening his eyes as he opened the car door for her.

Logic told her that he wasn't responsible for Miranda's appearance at the restaurant, but he was responsible for the fact that he had betrayed her father's trust and was now callously using her. How she hated him, loathed him, despised him!

She took a deep breath as she tried to close her mind against the unwelcome knowledge of just how much she herself hurt, how raw and painful her emotions felt. It was humiliating to know that he could still affect her like this, even now, as an adult.

Wrapped up in her thoughts, Imogen didn't realise that they had reached the house until Dracco leaned across her to open the car door. This close she could see the fine, soft hairs on his arm, see the taut structure of the sinew and muscle beneath his skin, smell the soap he used, clean and cool—and something else. Something that made her flesh come out in a rash of goosebumps, whilst her nostrils quivered with delicate female recognition of the potent maleness of his personal body scent, hot, musky and dangerous. Her eyes widened as she made an involuntary movement that somehow brought her body into immediate physical contact with his bare arm, her breasts pressing against it as though... Hot-faced, Imogen refused to acknowledge just what the insolent peaking of her nipples might be trying to proclaim as she pulled quickly back from him.

Ignoring him, she climbed out of the car, heading for the house. Behind her she could hear Dracco's footsteps crunching across the gravel. A sudden tremor of panic flared through her and she started to walk faster, only to realise that she couldn't get into the house without him, since she didn't possess a key.

Standing to one side, she waited for him to open the door. For the rest of her life she would hate him for what he was doing to her! Imogen could feel her hands balling into angry fists.

'Imo.'

Imogen felt Dracco's hands resting on her shoulders.

'Don't you dare touch me!' she spat furiously at him. But as she tried to pull away he refused to let her go, following the movement she made, so that she was backed up against the door.

'Imo, listen.'

'No.'

There was just time for Imogen to see the furious brilliant glitter of his eyes before his head blotted out the light as he grated angrily against her ear, 'Well, if you won't listen then perhaps this is the only way of communicating with you.'

She gasped once in outraged protest that he should dare to ignore her wishes, and then a second time, in shocked disbelief, as she felt the heat of his breath searing across her lips. And then she was not capable of gasping at all, as her breath was snatched away and with it her ability to think, and reason, and reject, because every fibre of her being, every single cell she possessed, was fully occupied in dealing with the nuclear fall-out caused by Dracco's kiss.

Its effect on her anger was like hot chocolate being poured on ice cream, she reflected dizzily, like every feeling, every pleasure, every delicious taste she had ever experienced magnified a million times over. It was like nothing she had ever dreamed of experiencing and at the same time it was exactly...exactly what she had always dreamed it might be, only more so...much more so.

Somehow the original furious anger of Dracco's kiss had turned to a sensuous, coaxing, lingering caress that involved not just their lips but their tongues as well. And their hands too, Imogen was discovering as her body melted beneath Dracco's touch, then burned, flamed and hungered...

'You kiss me like you've been aching for me for half a lifetime. Starving for me.' She could hear Dracco groaning as his hands ran fierce hot shudders of delight over her skin. He drew her body into his own, fitting her against him, fitting himself against her, into the cupped eagerness of her parted thighs.

As the full meaning of his words penetrated the sensual daze of her feelings Imogen suddenly realised what she was doing, and with a sharp cry she pulled away from him.

'I'm not starving—for anything, and certainly not for you,' she told him in passionate denial. 'But the street children of Rio are starving, Dracco, and that's why I'm here, because of them and only because of them.'

White-faced, she confronted him across the small space that now divided them.

His face was in the shadows, so that she could not see his expression, only sense his hunting immobility and know that he was watching her, making her feel vulnerable and exposed. She waited for him to voice some cutting put-down, but instead of retaliating in any way he simply turned from her and went to unlock the front door.

All the way up the stairs Imogen expected to hear him if not following her then at least commanding her to stop, but there was only silence. She didn't turn round to see why, though. She did not dare.

CHAPTER FOUR

IMOGEN was deeply asleep, lost in the most wonderful dream.

'Mmm.' Languorously she reached up to curl her hand against the firm, smooth skin at the nape of Dracco's neck. She could feel the silky thickness of his hair as she burrowed her fingertips into it, firmly drawing his head closer to her own.

'You know this is very dangerous, don't you?' Dracco was warning her in a sensually raw whisper, the sound caressing her skin with deliciously rough male warmth.

'I like danger,' Imogen responded provocatively as she looked up into the deep sea-green depths of his eyes. 'And I like it even more when that danger is you,' she added.

A small bubble of laughter gurgled in her throat as she saw the way Dracco was looking at her. It felt so good to be so at ease with him, so intimately aware of the special relationship they shared. At ease, and yet at the same time… A tiny thrill of wanton excitement shivered across her skin as she watched his eyes darken. Her own closed, her lips parting in eager anticipation of his kiss.

When it came the hot sweetness of it melted right through her body, touching every single nerve-ending, reaching into the deepest core of her, so that suddenly what they were doing was no longer a teasing game that she controlled, but a fierce, elemental need that controlled them both.

'Dracco!' Hungrily she reached out to drag him down against her naked body, driven to feel him against her, skin to skin, lips to lips, breath to breath! Helplessly her nails raked the firm flesh of his back as her body arched up against his, drawn into a tight, aching bow of longing.

As Dracco responded to her body's hungry demands he groaned her name against her lips. Imogen opened her eyes. Sunlight streamed in through her bedroom window, glinting on the gold of her wedding ring.

Dracco was holding her tightly now, his hands roving wantonly over her naked body with the powerful touch of a hungry sensualist, dipping lingeringly into her most secret places of delight, drawing from her a need to arouse him in the same way. Each kiss, each touch was taking her closer and closer to the shatteringly climactic culmination she knew was waiting for her, but as they did so somehow her joy was being overtaken by a fear that her happiness was about to be snatched away from her. A fear that made her cry out in anguish as she clung frantically to Dracco, desperately afraid that somehow she might lose him, lose his love.

'No!'

The sound of her own sharp moan of panic brought Imogen immediately out of her dream. For a few seconds she was still so wrapped up in it that it took her several deep breaths to realise just where she was. When she did she sat up in bed, reaching for her bedside light, illuminating the bedroom in a soft peachy glow. But nothing could warm the cold tentacles of dread reaching out to wrap themselves around her heart. She had been dreaming about Dracco, dreaming that he…that she… that they… Closing her eyes, Imogen hugged her arms around her body in an instinctive gesture of protection.

'Imogen, what's wrong? I heard you cry out.'

The sound of Dracco's voice as he thrust open her bedroom door and strode into her room made Imogen open her eyes immediately.

'Nothing. Nothing's wrong,' she denied tensely.

There was no way she could disclose to Dracco the content of her dream, nor exactly why she had given that anguished moan of distress.

'I heard you cry out,' Dracco persisted.

He was walking towards her bed as he spoke, and he was still fully dressed, although he had unbuttoned the top few buttons of his shirt and on the flesh they exposed Imogen could see the tangled criss-crossed darkness of his body hair.

Unable to drag her gaze away from it, she felt her stomach lurch. In her dream he had been totally naked. In her dream she had touched his skin, drawn her fingertips through that silky male covering of fine dark hair whilst her whole body quivered in thrilled sensual pleasure… Imogen shuddered.

What was happening to her? It had been years since she had fantasised about touching Dracco like that. She had been a mere girl then, sleeping in this very same bedroom. Was that it? Was it because she was sleeping in the room that had been hers as a girl that she had dreamed so inappropriately of the kind of intimacy with Dracco she most certainly no longer wanted? She was just beginning to relax into the security of finding a logical explanation for what had happened when she suddenly remembered how in her dream she had seen sunlight shining on her wedding ring.

A second shudder, even more apparent than her first, galvanised her body, bringing Dracco to the side of her bed, where he frowned down at her.

'Perhaps we should get Dr Armstrong to take a look at you,' he told her. 'You felt sick earlier on; now you're shivering.'

Imogen could feel her self-control starting to slip.

'There's nothing wrong with me. Apart from the fact that I'm being blackmailed into having sex with a man I don't want so that he can have the son he does want. But,' she added with angry sarcasm, 'I'm sure you aren't going to tell Dr Armstrong that. You're very good at not telling people things they ought to know, aren't you, Dracco?'

'And just what the hell do you mean?' he demanded.

'Work it out for yourself,' Imogen challenged him. When he continued to frown at her she flung at him bitterly, 'Somehow I don't imagine you've told Lisa about your plans for me. For the child you want me—*us*—to have,' she emphasised savagely. 'And…'

She took a deep breath, intending to remind him that he had also neglected to tell her, when he had originally proposed marriage to her, that he was already in love with her stepmother, but before she could do so he was interrupting her, exclaiming, 'No, I haven't. Why should I?'

How could he stand there and say that? Furiously Imogen confronted him.

'Why?' Imogen repeated in disbelief. Shaking her

head, she changed tack slightly, unable to trust herself to say what she was really feeling and settling instead for a quietly contemptuous, 'She's bound to find out, you know. Miranda will tell her.'

To her own shock she discovered that she was holding her breath, waiting, almost as though she was hoping that he would tell her Lisa was nothing to him now, that it was over between them. Was she really so frighteningly stupid, so crazily vulnerable?

'Our marriage, our relationship and the plans we make within it have nothing whatsoever to do with Lisa.'

'And you don't care what she thinks or feels about the situation?' Imogen challenged.

'My desire to have a child with your father's genes doesn't impact in any way at all on Lisa's life.'

'Nor on your relationship with her?' Imogen couldn't stop herself from persisting. There was a brief pause before Dracco answered.

'I know how you feel about Lisa, Imo, but you're an adult now. My relationship with her, as you term it, is what it is and cannot be changed. My feelings towards her haven't changed either, you know,' he told her as gently as he could.

Dracco frowned as he watched the look of anguished disbelief darkening Imogen's eyes. He knew how bitterly unhappy her stepmother had made her, and, as he had just told her, he liked Lisa as little now as he had done when John had first married her. In Dracco's eyes she was a shallow, selfish, greedy woman, but that did not alter the fact that, just as he had a responsibility towards Imogen, he also had a responsibility as one of the executors of Imogen's late father's will to ensure that Lisa received the biannual allowance she was entitled to. It was obvious, though, that Imogen was in no mood to listen to such logic.

Imogen felt as though someone was squeezing her lungs in a frighteningly painful grasp, making it almost impossible for her to breathe, but not impossible for her to feel. Oh, no, she could still do that! But why could she, when for the last four years she had believed that she no longer cared, that Dracco no longer had the power to hurt her, that her love for him had died along with her trust and respect?

'I think I hate you, Dracco,' she whispered savagely, correcting herself to tell him, 'No, I know I hate you.'

He was turning away from her and going to stand in front of her bedroom window, looking out into the darkness beyond it.

'Fine, you can hate me all you like,' he told her coolly, 'but you will still give me my son, Imo.'

Without giving her the opportunity to retaliate, he strode through her still open bedroom door, pulling it shut behind him.

As she glared at it, Imogen was not surprised to discover that she was shaking from head to foot—with burning hot rage. How could he; how dared he stand there and tell her he expected her to bear his child when he had just admitted that there was another woman in his life? And not just any 'other' woman, but her stepmother Lisa!

Of course, it was impossible for her to go back to sleep. A glance at her watch told her that it was only just gone midnight and she realised that Dracco must have heard her cry out on his own way to bed. How could she have allowed herself to dream about him like that? What part of her subconscious had produced those treacherous images? And why was the discovery that Dracco still loved Lisa making her feel not just that she wanted to hurl her furious contempt at him for his betrayal of her own youthful adoration, but also so filled with pain and despair?

Anyone would think that she still loved him, she derided herself warningly. And of course she did not!

If only she were back in Rio. There she had been safe; there she had been far too busy to think about Dracco. She made a small restless movement in her bed as her conscience prodded her for the lie she was telling herself. 'All right, then,' she muttered beneath her breath, 'so I did think about him occasionally.'

You thought about him and you dreamed about him, that same voice reminded her relentlessly. You know you did.

'Yes, yes, all right,' she conceded, 'but those were not dreams, they were nightmares, and I had quite definitely stopped loving him. Quite definitely!

'You've got half an hour to have breakfast and then we're leaving for London.'

As she heard what Dracco was saying to her for a moment Imogen's hopes rose. Had he changed his mind after what she had said to him last night? Was he taking her back to London in order to put her on a plane to Rio?

Oh, please...please! she begged fate fervently as she

told Dracco automatically, 'I don't eat breakfast. I'll go up and pack.'

'Pack?' Dracco's eyebrows lifted as he drawled the single word laconically, shaking his head as he did so. 'We're going to see our solicitor, Imo, and it won't involve an overnight stay, although I dare say you might want to wear something a little more formal,' he added as he flicked a disparaging glance at her well-worn outfit.

Immediately Imogen was on the defensive. 'If you don't like my clothes, Dracco—' she began, and then was forced to stop, as without allowing her to finish Dracco cut in smoothly,

'I can buy you some new ones? My feelings exactly, Imo, and that's what I intend to do, once our business with David is concluded. I don't doubt that you trust me, just as I do you, but I thought it might give you some degree of reassurance if I committed myself legally to our…agreement. I intend to take your adherence to your part on trust. What do you mean, you don't eat breakfast?' he suddenly questioned her with a frown.

The lightning speed with which he changed subjects threw Imogen into total confusion. And distracted her from the shock of discovering that he intended to put the proposal he had made to her on a legal footing.

The proposal he had made to her? The blackmail he was forcing on her, she corrected herself fiercely as she heard him saying, 'No wonder you're so slender. Have some of these.'

Imogen's eyes widened as he reached out and picked up a packet of cereal from the table, shaking some into the bowl in front of her.

'Fruit Munchies with chocolate chips,' he told her humorously. 'You used to love them.'

'That was when I was thirteen,' Imogen reminded him, but Dracco wasn't paying any attention.

Instead he poured milk onto her cereal, before warning her, 'We don't leave this house until you have eaten, Imo.'

'Why? Are you afraid that people will think you're starving me as well as blackmailing me?' she demanded acerbically.

'Blackmailing you?' He gave her a sharply incisive look, but before he could continue the telephone started to ring. 'Excuse me,' he told her. 'This is probably a business call I was expecting. I'll take it in the study. I shan't be long.'

After he had gone Imogen stared at the bowl in front of her. She wasn't going to eat the cereal, of course she wasn't, but somehow she was dipping her spoon into it. In Rio she had eaten sparingly, knowing how little food the children they were dealing with had to eat.

She was over halfway through by the time Dracco returned, and, although she pushed the bowl away from her without finishing its contents, she had to admit that she had rather enjoyed the cereal.

Dracco's solicitor had an office in the same block that housed the offices which had originally been her father's and which were now, of course, exclusively Dracco's.

A sharp pang gripped Imogen as she remembered how often she had visited the office with her father. She still missed him, not with the savage intensity she had suffered immediately after his death any longer, but with a sadness that had become a small, familiar shadow in her life.

As he guided her towards the lift Dracco said quietly to her, 'I've lost count of the number of times I've thought about moving. I still expect to see your father here, coming out of the lift, opening the office door. I still miss him and I dare say I always will.'

His words were so in tune with her thoughts that Imogen couldn't speak without betraying her emotions. Instead she turned her face away from Dracco so that he couldn't see it. How could he speak so about her father and yet at the same time have betrayed him by falling in love with his wife?

Imogen continued to ignore Dracco as the lift bore them upwards. When it stopped and the door opened he touched her arm, and immediately Imogen flinched.

Despairingly she wondered how on earth she would be able to keep her part of the bargain and provide him with a child when she couldn't even bear him to touch her!

You managed to bear it very well when he kissed you last night, a small inner voice told her, adding, 'And what about that dream? Then you weren't just bearing it.

'No,' Imogen protested out loud, covering her ears with her hands.

'What is it?' Dracco demanded sharply. Are you feeling ill again? I really do think you need to be checked out by Dr Armstrong. You could have picked up something on the flight.'

'I'm fine,' Imogen choked. She could see an office door ahead of them.

There was still time for her to change her mind. Still time for her to decide that she was not strong enough to make such a sacrifice and to fly straight back to Rio. All it would take was one sentence, but even whilst she longed to speak it, to tell Dracco that she had changed her mind, Imogen's pride refused to allow her to do so. Her pride and the deep inner knowledge that she would never forgive herself for her selfishness if she did.

Dracco pushed open the office door, ushering her inside ahead of him. A smiling receptionist greeted them. It was obvious that she knew Dracco well and was more than a touch in awe of him.

'David shouldn't be long,' she told Dracco, glancing at her watch. 'He was called out to a meeting with a client. He didn't want to go, really, knowing that you were coming in, but it was an urgent case.'

She seemed almost to be apologising, Imogen recognised as the other woman turned to smile a little uncertainly at her. She was about her own age, Imogen guessed, brunette with hazel eyes and very obviously pregnant.

Shakily Imogen averted her gaze from the other woman's body. She was still saying something to Dracco, but then she stopped as the office door opened and a slightly thick-set young man with an open, honest face came in.

'Oh, there you are, darling,' she said with obvious relief. 'I was just explaining to Dracco that you'd had to go out.'

As she reached up to kiss him briefly Imogen noticed the wedding ring she was wearing and guessed that they were husband and wife even before Dracco had introduced them to her as David and Charlotte Bryant.

'Mrs Barrington.' David Bryant smiled as he shook Imogen's hand. 'I've heard an awful lot about you. My uncle Henry was a great fan of yours and of course he and your father were very close friends. He often used to talk to my mother about you. She was his sister. I know how much it would have meant to him to learn that you and Dracco are...have decided... That you are reconciled.' He stopped, colouring up and looking slightly uncomfortable, whilst Imogen automatically asked him to call her by her Christian name. It irked her that Dracco had been so sure of her reaction that he had already told David Bryant that they were 'reconciled'.

She must not allow herself to forget that Dracco was a master manipulator, she warned herself as she thanked Charlotte Bryant for the cup of coffee she had just made her.

'Yes,' the other woman was confirming quietly, 'David's mother often talks about her brother to us. I know she is particularly grateful to you, Dracco, for everything you did when he had his fatal heart attack, going with him to the hospital, staying with him.'

'It was the least I could do,' Imogen heard Dracco saying curtly, almost as though he didn't want the subject to be discussed.

Imogen shivered. If Henry had not had his heart attack, would Dracco have come after her and stopped her from leaving? She had believed he had let her go out of indifference and relief, but now it seemed that she might have been wrong. Had she been wrong about anything else?

David and Charlotte Bryant obviously thought a lot of Dracco, but then they didn't know him the way she did!

'So what now? A celebratory glass of champagne? We aren't too far from one of the city's new hotels, and, since it's time for lunch...'

Imogen stared at Dracco in disbelief as they stepped out of the office block and into the sunshine.

'You might feel you have something to celebrate,' she told him wildly, 'but I most certainly don't.'

'No? I've just signed a legally binding document agreeing to give your charity over one million pounds. I should have thought that was sufficient cause for celebration,' Dracco was telling her with deceptive mildness as he caught hold of her arm and drew her against his side.

Immediately Imogen tried to pull away, but Dracco refused to let go of her.

'That might be—under different circumstances,' Imogen retaliated, 'but, since I've just sold the use of my body to you in return for it...'

She could see Dracco's mouth thinning and see too the warning glint in his rapidly darkening eyes.

'You loved your father, didn't you, Imo?' he asked her grimly.

'You know I did,' Imogen responded immediately.

'How do you think he would have reacted to being a grandfather, to knowing that his genes, your mother's and your own were being passed on to a new generation?'

For a moment Imogen was too shaken by his question

to answer, but when she did her voice trembled with the intensity of her feelings.

'How dare you do this to me, Dracco?' she demanded. 'How dare you use my father to blackmail me?'

'You keep throwing that accusation in my face. Be very careful that I don't throw it back at you.'

'By doing what?' she challenged him recklessly.

But instead of answering her he said calmly, 'Since you don't want any lunch, we might as well head straight for Knightsbridge and get you kitted out with some new clothes.'

'I don't want any new clothes,' Imogen started to say, but Dracco wasn't listening to her, his attention concentrated on the taxi he was hailing.

He was still holding onto Imogen's arm, his fingers curling firmly around it, and as a group of passers-by jostled against her she automatically moved closer to him. The cool wool of his suit jacket brushed against her bare arm. As she looked up she could see the faint shadow on his jaw where he had shaved earlier. There was a maleness about Dracco, she acknowledged with a faint inner tremor, a strong, dangerous sense of power that was like an unseen aura. Unseen but not unfelt. She could feel it now as he urged her into the stationary taxi. She could feel it and she was afraid of it—and of herself.

'And just remember,' Dracco was warning her as the taxi lurched into motion, 'from tonight you and I will be sharing a bedroom. And a bed.'

Ignoring him, Imogen stared out of the taxi window, praying that she would get pregnant quickly—no, not just quickly but immediately, she amended hurriedly.

Straight away, the first time, so that it would be the

only time. Would Dracco wait to see if…? Or would he…? Her mind shied away from the questions bubbling inside her head. She certainly had no fear of sex as such. These were not, after all, Victorian times, when a virgin bride was simply not told anything about what lay ahead of her. In Rio children well below the age of puberty sold themselves on the streets in order to eat and were shockingly graphic about what could be demanded of them. If providing Dracco with a child saved only one of those children…

Dracco's child. Her child. Unable to stop herself, Imogen turned to look at him. Just as she had been, he was gazing out of the taxi window, his face averted from her. Imogen cleared her throat to speak but did not get the chance. The taxi was drawing up outside a department store.

'No, that's enough—more than enough,' Imogen protested helplessly as she surveyed the full rail of clothes the store's senior personal shopper had produced.

They—Dracco, herself, the shopper and a hovering alterationist—were all in the store's elegant personal shopping suite, where Dracco and Imogen had been escorted following Dracco's production of a discreetly logoed charge card and request for a selection of clothes for Imogen to choose from.

Initially dizzy from the mouth-watering variety of outfits the personal shopper had produced, Imogen was now beginning to feel slightly nauseous in a way that reminded her of how her teenage self had sometimes felt after the consumption of a mega-sized knickerbocker glory.

Tempting though the clothes were, Imogen's conscience was causing her to experience a sense of disquiet. Just how many small stomachs would the cost of such luxurious clothes fill? And thinking of stomachs, small and otherwise, raised another consideration…

Yearningly Imogen looked at the trendy pair of designer jeans she had just tried on. The assistant had explained how they were cut to fit and flatter the female body, and they had hugged Imogen's hips and bottom in a way that had made her reluctant to come out of the cubicle until the shopper had insisted. When she had done, she'd felt acutely self-conscious standing in front of Dracco wearing them, guessing what he must be thinking—that they were far too sexy for a woman like her!

'They're not really me,' she said now, shaking her head, but Dracco, it seemed, had other ideas.

'Why not?' he asked her. 'I like them.' As he spoke Imogen was infuriatingly aware of the disparaging look he was giving the outfit she had put back on.

Lisa had always worn very fashionable, sexy clothes, and no doubt as he looked at her Dracco was mentally comparing her to his mistress.

Did he perhaps think that by dressing her in sexy clothes she would somehow become more desirable to him, more the kind of woman he wanted?

Imogen had never forgotten the disparaging comments Lisa had made to her on the morning of her marriage, and somehow since then she had favoured loose-fitting clothes that cloaked rather than emphasised her figure.

'They're very popular—and very sexy.' The shopper was smiling encouragingly.

Until he had decided that he wanted a child with her Dracco had shown no sexual interest in her whatsoever. Before their marriage he had never even kissed her properly, and yet now he apparently wanted to buy her the kind of clothes that subtly enhanced a woman's sexuality. Why? Because that would make her more acceptable to him in bed? More like Lisa?

'No,' she insisted, ignoring the jeans the shopper was still holding. 'They're very expensive and I wouldn't get much wear out of them.'

'We'll take them.' Dracco was smiling as he spoke to the assistant. 'If it's that social conscience of yours that's troubling you,' he told Imogen as he turned towards her, 'then let me remind you that it's my money you'll be spending, and…'

'Your money?' Immediately Imogen started to frown, anger taking the place of her earlier self-consciousness. 'I can afford to buy my own clothes, Dracco,' she told him fiercely. 'I did have a salary for my work for the charity, albeit a small one!'

Discreetly the personal shopper had moved out of earshot.

'I know you can,' Dracco agreed, 'but surely it's a husband's privilege to be allowed to indulge his wife?'

Thoroughly angry now, Imogen glared at him. 'If you really want to "indulge me", as you put it, there are other ways!'

To her disbelief, she could see that Dracco was actually starting to smile.

'You haven't really changed at all, have you, Imo?' he challenged her ruefully. 'I can remember how much it amused your father—and infuriated Lisa—when you insisted that you'd rather he bought some winter feed for the ponies tethered illegally on the village common than buy you a Christmas-party dress.'

To her own mortification, Imogen felt emotional tears start to prick the backs of her eyes.

Yes, she could remember that incident as well. Her father had been amused, and in the end she had not only got his agreement to provide winter feed for the ponies, but she had also, at Lisa's furious insistence, got a new party dress as well. She had hated that dress, it had been babyish, pink, with frills and a big full skirt, not suitable for a teenager at all.

Lisa—was Dracco thinking of her now? Was he wishing that Lisa was here with him; that she was the one he was buying a new wardrobe for that she would wear for his delectation—both in bed and out of it? Imogen forced herself to take a deep, calming breath.

'Anyway,' she told Dracco, 'there isn't much point in you buying me these kind of clothes.' When Dracco raised one eyebrow interrogatively she flushed a little as she was forced to explain huskily, 'They're all very fitted, and I won't… I shan't… I shall probably soon be needing things with more room in them,' she told him, unable to stop herself from giving him an indignant look when the enlightenment finally dawned in his eyes.

'If you're trying to say that you'll soon be needing maternity outfits, then, yes, I agree,' he said in obvious amusement. 'But I think our reconciliation alone is going to cause enough speculation without us adding to it by you appearing in public in maternity gear.' Giving her an oblique look, he added softly, 'I must say, you've surprised me, Imo; I hadn't realised you were so actively looking forward to the consummation of our agreement!'

'That isn't what I meant. I'm not!' Imogen hissed in immediate denial. She couldn't believe his sudden and unexpected lightheartedness. It was almost as though he was teasing her, and enjoying doing so as well. 'I just don't want to see money being wasted on clothes that—'

'Will it make you feel better if I agree to match pound for pound everything I spend on you with an additional donation to the shelter?' Dracco asked.

Imogen opened her mouth and then closed it again. She didn't want to see him like this, to remember how wonderful and special she had once believed he was. To make up for her own foolish weakness she gave him a mutely hostile look before telling him frostily, 'That's bribery.'

'It's your decision,' Dracco replied. 'Just remember that the less you spend on yourself, the less I give to the shelter.'

The personal shopper was moving determinedly back towards them, obviously having decided that they had had enough time to sort out their differences. Was there anything Dracco would not do to get his own way? Imogen wondered helplessly.

Whether it was because of Dracco's comment, the personal shopper's skilled salesmanship, or her own unexpected pleasure in the clothes she tried on, Imogen didn't know, but when she finally left the suite she was the slightly guilty owner of a much larger new wardrobe than she had planned—and the shelter was in line to get a substantial extra 'bonus'.

'I take it that on this occasion you won't want to celebrate a successful conclusion to our activities at the Soda Fountain,' Dracco drawled as they left the store with half a dozen large carrier bags.

For some reason, his reference to a favourite rendezvous for her schoolgirl treats on her visits to her father's office filled her with a welling sense of emotion. So much so that she stopped dead in the street, causing Dracco's smile to change to a frown as he watched her.

Imogen felt as though she wanted to run and hide.

Just for one betraying millisecond of time she had caught herself actually wishing that things could be different, that she and Dracco were genuinely making an attempt to start afresh with one another and that the planned conception of their child, her father's grandchild, was an event they were undertaking in a mutual mood of love and joy.

What on earth was happening to her? Did it really only take the mention of the Soda Fountain to wipe away the betrayals that lay between them? Surely she wasn't really so foolish and so vulnerable?

Her head lifted, her pride responding to the challenge she had given it. Managing a valiant smile, she told Dracco coolly, 'Somehow I doubt that indulging in calorie-laden snacks and these clothes—' she swung her carrier bags meaningfully '—go together.'

'You could do with putting a bit of weight on,' Dracco informed her, still frowning.

Of course he would think that! Lisa was far more voluptuously shaped than she was. 'Well, if you have your way I expect I soon shall be,' Imogen returned, and then caught her bottom lip in her teeth, her face burning a hot, self-conscious pink.

For a moment Dracco said nothing, simply studying her with a hooded gaze whilst more than one woman passer-by paused to look interestedly at him.

'If that's meant to be an invitation—' he began.

Immediately Imogen stopped him, shaking her head vigorously as she denied any such intention. 'The day I invite you to take me to bed,' she told him furiously, 'is—'

'Be careful, Imo,' Dracco told her softly. 'I've already warned you about challenging me.'

CHAPTER FIVE

ALMOST childishly Imogen kept her eyes tightly closed, even though she had been awake for well over ten minutes, knowing already what she would see the moment she opened them.

Outside the bedroom window she could hear a blackbird carolling noisily. Fighting to ignore the sensation of despair in the pit of her stomach, Imogen opened her eyes and stared across her pillow to the one that should have borne the imprint of Dracco's dark head. But, just like the huge double bed itself, it showed no evidence of Dracco's presence.

It was five days now since they had returned from London, almost a week, and still nothing had happened; still Dracco had not...they had not...

All right, so he had been away on business for three of those nights, but she had moved into the master suite the evening of their return from the shopping trip filled with trepidation. Dracco had never come anywhere near the room, or her, preferring instead to sleep downstairs on the sofa in his study, apparently because he was in the middle of a very important business deal which necessitated him making and receiving calls from other continents.

'There was no point in me coming upstairs and disturbing you, not when I knew I'd got these calls coming through,' he had explained carelessly to her the next day when she had eventually seen him. 'You weren't disappointed, I hope?'

Imogen had not known what to reply. And she had told herself that she was only too pleased to hear that he would be going away for a few days.

But in his absence, no doubt because she had had the unfamiliar luxury of time to think about such things, she had found herself questioning just why he had not as yet made any attempt to ensure that she gave him the child he wanted; the child that was, after all, the reason for them being here together.

Yesterday, when he had returned without warning late in the afternoon, she had been convinced that the event she was dreading was imminent, but once again Dracco had left her to sleep alone.

Because he didn't want her? Because he only wanted the child she could give him? Because in reality the woman he truly wanted was Lisa?

The pristine pillow next to her own began to blur. Wrathfully Imogen told herself that she didn't care and blinked away the tears. She was not going to cry!

No, instead of wanting to cry she ought to be asking herself why she was being so illogical. After all, by rights she should have been pleased.

Once she had showered and dressed, Imogen made her way downstairs. She had grown up in this house. Absently she ran her fingertips along the smooth rich wood of the carved banister rail. Hidden in its carving were tiny little animals; Imogen could remember her mother showing them to her. When her mother had been alive this house had been a home, the kind of home she would have wanted to give her own child, but her mother's death and her father's remarriage had changed that and had turned it into a place she had needed to seek refuge from.

And the person she had sought that refuge with most often had been Dracco! Dracco. Where was he? The study door was closed. Tentatively Imogen hovered outside it and then, taking a deep breath, she reached for the handle and turned it.

Inside the room the computer hummed softly, its screen illuminating the semi-darkness. Frowning, her housewifely instincts aroused, Imogen started to make her way towards the window to release the closed blind and let the sunlight in, but then, abruptly, she stopped as she saw Dracco's sleeping form sprawled uncomfortably on the narrow sofa.

He was still wearing the clothes he had arrived home in the previous afternoon—a lightweight suit, the jacket of which was lying on a chair. At some stage he had obviously started to unbutton his shirt, and as her eyes adjusted to the half-light of the room Imogen could see the deep dark 'V' of exposed flesh stretching from his throat all the way down to where his trousers lay low on his hips.

Her muscles contracted in helpless reaction, a silent, tortured contortion that sliced through her body. She made an involuntary movement towards him and then stopped. In the shuttered heat of the room his fine, silky body hair lay in damp whorls against his flesh; his chest rose and fell with his breathing. Even relaxed, his muscles had an imposing male tautness that drew and held her gaze. Once, as a girl, she had yearned to touch

Dracco's body, her imagination, her senses, her deepest self driven crazy with excitement and longing.

In Rio, whenever she had fallen into the trap of thinking about Dracco, or remembering how she had felt about him, she had told herself sternly that her imaginings had been those of a hormone-fevered adolescent with no bearing whatsoever on reality. She had assured herself too that as an adult she would look scornfully on the reactions of the girl she had been, that she would be safely beyond such foolish feelings.

She had been wrong, Imogen recognised dizzily. Right now the effect the sight of Dracco was having on her was—

'Imo?'

Imogen jumped as though she had been stung as Dracco suddenly said her name. How long had he been awake, watching her watching him? Guilty heat stained her skin and she started to back towards the door.

'I...I wasn't sure if you were in here,' she began huskily.

'I had some work to do,' Dracco told her casually as he sat up and grimaced slightly as he flexed his body. 'I remember feeling tired.'

'It can't have been very comfortable for you, sleeping on the sofa,' Imogen told him.

She barely knew what she was saying; all she could think about was the extraordinary and very definitely unwanted surge of feeling that had filled her whilst she had been looking at him.

'Mmm...it could have been worse,' Dracco responded.

For some reason the way he was looking at her made

her face burn even hotter. What exactly was he implying? That sleeping on the sofa was preferable to sleeping with her? He was the one who had insisted that he didn't want their marriage annulled! Imogen turned round and reached for the door handle.

She was opening the door when Dracco said abruptly from behind her, 'If you like we could go out later. Drive to the coast?'

Once such an invitation would have filled her with incandescent joy, and no power on earth would have prevented her from accepting it. Perhaps it was because she could remember that feeling so vividly that she felt she had to punish herself. Imogen didn't know, but she could hear the anger and the pain in her voice as she replied pointedly, shaking her head, 'No, I don't like. There's only one reason I'm here, Dracco, and it doesn't have anything to do with trips to the coast.'

She was gone before he could retaliate, closing the door behind her as she hurried into the kitchen.

A solitary morning followed by an afternoon deadheading roses had not done anything to improve her mood, Imogen recognised as she sucked irritably on her thorn-pricked thumb while hurrying upstairs.

'Imo.'

She froze as Dracco suddenly appeared at the top of the stairs. He was virtually naked, a towel wrapped casually around his hips whilst he rubbed absently at his wet hair with another.

'I saw you coming in from the garden from the bedroom window,' he began, 'and I thought—'

'That you ought to warn me that you were wandering

around half-naked, just in case I got the wrong idea?' Imogen supplied grittily for him. 'You were the one who threatened to seduce me, Dracco, not the other way around,' she couldn't resist pointing out.

'Actually, what I wanted to discuss with you is the fact that you're going to need some form of transport. I was thinking perhaps of a small four-wheel drive. They seem very popular with mothers.' His voice dropped to a dangerous softness that brought up the hairs on the nape of Imogen's neck in sensual awareness as intensely as though he had physically reached out and touched her, when he added smoothly, 'However, since you have raised the subject...'

'I have not raised anything,' Imogen objected immediately, and then went bright red, whilst Dracco continued to look at her with that detached hooded gaze of his that was so unreadable.

'And am I to take that as an indication that you do want to raise...something?' Dracco queried dangerously gently.

'You're the one who insisted that our marriage was to continue and that...you wanted me to...that you wanted a child,' Imogen told him wildly.

'And if I remember correctly you were the one who said that there was no point in me attempting to seduce you,' Dracco pointed out. 'However, if you're trying to tell me that you've changed your mind...?'

Changed her mind? No! Never! She would die before she did that! But for some reason Imogen found it impossible to voice that fierce denial. Perhaps, she decided, it was because her attention was concentrated not on her own thoughts but on the precarious way in which Dracco had wrapped the towel around his hips, so loosely that…

Imogen discovered that she couldn't drag her fascinated gaze away from it. And nor, it seemed, could she resist allowing that same gaze to skim helplessly over the flat muscular plane of Dracco's belly with its dark arrowing of hair that disappeared beneath the soft whiteness of his towel. She found that, as badly as she wanted to swallow, for some reason she could not.

'Imo.'

There was a smooth, liquid sensuality in the way Dracco mouthed her name, a spellbinding dark magic that somehow paralysed her so that she couldn't move until his fingers curled round her wrist as he firmly tugged her towards him.

'You smell of fresh air and sunshine,' she heard him whisper against her hair. 'And roses.'

'You smell of…you,' Imogen whispered helplessly back. Her eyes, already huge in the delicate triangle of her face, widened even further when she saw the look that leapt fiercely to life in Dracco's own eyes. The look of a hunter, a male animal, aroused, dangerous, silently waiting to pounce.

'Have you any idea just how provocative that remark is?' he asked her with a soft savagery that made her whole body shudder.

As she shook her head he mouthed her denial for her, questioning, 'No?' His hand moved to hold the side of her neck, tipping it back, his thumb rimming the shape of her ear, sending a shower of pleasure darting over her skin. The warmth of his breath as he bent his head towards her scorched her senses. His fingers, stroking the delicate, sensitive flesh just beneath her hairline, made her tremble wildly without knowing why she should do so.

'You don't know just what it does to a man when you tell him that you can recognise his personal scent? Shall I tell you? Show you?'

He had closed the distance between them, enclosing her with his body, so that she could feel its heat—and more. Automatically she tensed against her awareness of his arousal, a virgin's shocked reaction to a man's sexuality, but beneath that reaction, running hot and wild, was a river of flooding sensation.

'No.' Her denial slid from her lips into the infinitesimal space between them, and was lost for ever as Dracco's mouth brushed hers—the briefest of touches, and yet somehow so sensual and commanding that Imogen automatically felt her toes starting to curl.

'More? You want more?' she heard Dracco murmuring, even though she could have sworn she had said nothing. Perhaps it was her body that had given her away, her lips? 'Like this, Imo?' Dracco was asking her, his voice so soft and low that she had to strain to hear it, just as she was having to strain to reach out for the feel of his mouth against her own. 'Your mouth should taste sweet and virginal and not all dark enchantment, the mouth of a sorceress no man can resist. Are you a sorceress, Imo?'

Dizzily Imogen tried to listen to what he was saying, but there was a sharp, fierce ache in her body. Beneath her thin top she could feel her breasts swelling, her nipples tight, hurting with the need to have Dracco touch them, stroke them, suck them.

She shuddered wildly, her eyes suddenly wantonly feral as her female instincts overwhelmed her. It was as though time had telescoped backwards, as though somehow she was feeling once again what she had felt as a teenager, only now she was feeling those desires and needs with all the authority and power of a truly mature woman.

Somehow, too, her body considered Dracco to be its mate, a mate from whom it had been parted for far too long! Denied far too long!

Urgently she wound her arms around Dracco's body, holding him to her, her gaze smouldering passionately into his.

'Do you want me?' he asked her softly. 'When, Imo?' he demanded when her body shuddered in response. 'Now?'

Imogen felt her body jolt against his as though it had received a charge of electricity. 'Yes,' she responded hoarsely. 'Yes, now,' she told him. 'Now, Dracco!' she repeated urgently, raising herself up on her tiptoes and pressing her mouth passionately against his.

For a second there was no response, and then Dracco opened his mouth on hers, the fierce drive of his tongue into the intimate sweetness she was willingly offering shattering all her teenage preconceptions about what such a kiss would be.

It was like drowning, dying, being turned inside-out, giving something of herself so intimate that she felt as though he was totally possessing her, and yet at the same time filling her with such an aching hunger that she felt as though she would die unless he satisfied it. And she knew only he, only Dracco alone, could satisfy her.

Beneath her hands she could feel the sleek, hard warmth of his bare skin, the breadth of his shoulders tapering down into the narrowness of his waist. The barrier of his towel frustrated her and beneath the increasingly demanding thrust of Dracco's seeking tongue she made a small, angry sound of protest.

Immediately he released her, staring down into the desire-hazed darkness of her eyes with a gaze so green and luminous that it made her heart turn over.

'What is it?' he asked her rawly. 'Too much—too soon?'

He was holding one of her hands in his own, and as she turned away, unable to answer his question, his fingers suddenly tightened almost painfully on hers, causing her to look quickly back at him.

'This doesn't say that you don't want me, Imo,' he told her, and her breath caught on a frantic gasp of mingled shock and pleasure as he ran his fingertip over the jutting outline of her breast, pausing deliberately to circle her nipple, erect and aroused beneath the fine fabric of her top.

Without waiting for her to answer him, he turned towards the master suite, firmly drawing her with him. Imogen didn't try to resist. She didn't want to resist.

The bedroom was dappled with evening sunlight; it shone through the voile curtaining, giving the peaceful cream comfort of the room a golden gleam.

As a new extension to the original house, this room did not share the air of sad shabbiness that had so struck at Imogen's emotions when she had first walked into her childhood home. In her parents' day this room had simply not existed, and Imogen acknowledged her sense of relief and release that this bedroom held no painful memories for her, and that she was coming to it as an adult woman.

'This room suits you, Imo,' Dracco was telling her quietly whilst his thumb ran lazily up and down the inside of her bare arm, the effect of his touch on her so devastatingly erotic that she found it almost impossible to focus on what he was saying.

'Cream is your colour. Cream and gold.' He leaned forward, his lips caressing the side of her neck, his fingers so swift and deft on the fastening of her top that she was barely aware of the fact that he had slid it off her shoulder until she felt the heat of his mouth caressing her there.

A hundred thousand fiery darts of pleasure thrilled over her skin. She heard the sound of her own low, aching moan filling the room; a counterpoint to the rapidly increasing rate of their breathing.

Dracco's hands were sliding beneath her top, easing it off her body. A delicious shivery sensation shimmered over her skin.

'Cream, and honey-gold,' Imogen heard Dracco saying thickly as he freed her breasts from the confines of her bra and gently kneaded them, playing tenderly with the stiff peaks of her nipples in a way that made her writhe hotly in his embrace. She closed her eyes and bit into her bottom lip as she fought to suppress the raw moan of appreciative delight she could feel building up inside her.

'Beautiful! You are so very beautiful, even more perfect than I knew. So perfect that I can hardly bear to look at you. Do you know what it does to me, Imo, seeing you like this?' she could hear Dracco demanding as he looked down at her naked breasts and then back up into her eyes.

The expression she could see in the depths of those eyes both shocked and thrilled her.

Dracco wanted her. She could see it; feel it in his body; hear it in his voice.

That knowledge was all she needed to loosen the last faint threads of inhibition binding her and set herself free to be the woman she had always known she could be—with Dracco.

As his hands came to her waist, so narrow that her trousers slid down from it to lie loosely on her hips, Imogen raised herself up on her tiptoes. She still wasn't quite brave enough to look down at Dracco's body. Miraculously his towel was still in place, but he had not made any attempt to disguise how aroused he was.

When she reached to wrap her arms around him Dracco held her slightly away from him. He whispered thickly, 'Let me see all of you, Imo.'

Although his words made her tremble, she didn't try to resist as he carefully removed her trousers, unzipping them to let them fall to the floor and then lifting her out of them, holding her right there against his own body. She was pressed deep into his hard masculinity, thigh to thigh, hip to hip, groin to groin, whilst he kissed her with a slow passion that burned and smouldered potently.

Imogen ached to open her legs and wrap them tightly around him, to lure and coax him by any means she could to take the gift she was so wantonly ready to give him. Just the thought of feeling him sliding powerfully into her was enough to make her shudder again wildly, her eyes stormily dark with longing.

How could she have lived so long without this, without him? It was a question she couldn't even begin to answer.

Mutely she let him slide her down to the floor, his hands smoothing the flesh of her back, her waist, her buttocks, cupping the soft feminine cheeks, his fingers splayed over them.

Imogen could hear the frantic high-pitched sound of her sharp protest that he should arouse her so intensely and tormentingly without satisfying her, but it was something she heard from a distance, her whole being concentrated on the increasingly urgent necessity of feeling him, having him touch her with the full intimacy of a lover.

Her nails clawed his naked back, echoing the intensity of what she was feeling. Impatiently she tugged at the soft fabric of the towel covering his body.

Against her ear she could hear him asking, 'Imo, are you sure this is what you want? Because if it isn't and you don't tell me now…'

How could he even ask her such a question? Couldn't he tell? See? Feel?

'I want you, Dracco,' she told him. 'I want you now.'

It was like nothing she had ever imagined, and so much—so much more than everything she had ever dared to hope for. Tears of emotion stung her eyes at the look on Dracco's face as he studied her naked body, his gaze absorbed, hungry, fiercely hungry, in direct contrast to the tender touch of his hands.

When he kissed her breasts, each one in turn and then

each nipple, slowly laving the aching peaks, she shivered in mute ecstasy. The slow trail of his tongue-tip down over her belly had the same effect on her skin as red wine might have had on her blood—a hot, sensual rush of pleasure that took control of her senses. To call the effect he was having on her mind-blowing fell so far short of the reality of what he was doing to her that it was almost an insult. When his tongue rimmed her navel, and dipped gently into it, she moaned out loud in bewildered pleasure.

Never in a thousand lifetimes had she imagined this kind of intimacy with him, and never had it even crossed her mind that she would be the one urging him on with her hands, with the hoarse cry of her voice and with the frantic writhing of her body. Through her half-closed eyes she could still see the full, powerful maleness of him. She ached to reach out and touch him, but the sensation of him gently parting the outer covering of her sex made her forget everything but her intense need for him.

Instincts she hadn't known she possessed were driving her, possessing her now, insisting that the mere touch of his fingers was not enough, not what her body really needed, even though their careful touch was making her shudder from head to foot.

'Dracco,' she whispered, pleading.

Immediately he was beside her, looking deep into her eyes as he demanded hoarsely, 'What is it? Do you want me to stop?'

'No, it isn't that,' Imogen denied immediately. Helplessly her gaze, hot and fevered with longing, jolted over his body. 'I want you, Dracco,' she told him fiercely. 'You... With me. Inside me.'

For a moment the triumphant blaze in his eyes shocked her. It was as though she had said something, given him something he had hungered for for a very long time. But it was too late to try to analyse what she thought she might have seen; Dracco was gathering her up in his arms, holding her, positioning her, moving over her and then finally and oh, so blissfully into her.

The high, wild sound of her cry of longing mingled with the harshly guttural groan of Dracco's male growl of possession. Their bodies moved together in an urgent harmony that felt so right, so natural that it seemed to Imogen she had finally found a vitally important missing piece of her life and herself.

And then there was no room for thought, no room for anything other than absorbing the feel of Dracco's body, the hot, musky scent of his skin, the physical reality of him here with her and within her as he drove them both to that place she knew she would die if she did not reach it.

But she did reach it, reached it and exploded in a million tiny pieces of piercingly intense release to lie exhausted in Dracco's protective arms. She was dazed with satisfaction and an awed disbelief that it was possible to experience something so spectacularly wonderful as sleep claimed her.

CHAPTER SIX

IMOGEN opened her eyes and stretched luxuriously. Dracco might not still be in the bed beside her but she could still smell his scent, feel the warm place where his body had been, feel the secret, special, place within herself where he had been.

Rolling over, she looked towards the window. It was a wonderful day. How could it not be? The revelations of the previous night still clung to her, filling her emotions with the same golden glow the sun brought through the window, its brightness softened into a mellow gilding by the voile curtains.

And so it was with her own feelings; they too were softened, gilded by the wondrous power of love, the love she had rediscovered in the breathless passages of the night when Dracco had held her, touching not just her body and her senses but also the deepest and most precious part of her.

They might not have spoken of love, but they had breathed it, shared it, given and bequeathed it to one another, surely? There was no way she could be mistaken about that.

She turned her head and studied the pillow next to her own, the pillow that still bore the imprint of Dracco's head. It was a new and sweet thing for her, this soft heaviness within her body, this small ache of satisfaction and remembered pleasure.

She had so many plans for her future, their future; so many hopes. Joy trembled uncertainly within her. She didn't want to question what she was feeling, nor to analyse the past. She didn't, Imogen recognised, want anything to intrude on the special memories and pleasures she and Dracco had created together.

She and Dracco together…

And perhaps, just perhaps, memories weren't all they had created!

A fierce quickening sensation gripped her body. A child.

'I want your father's grandchild,' Dracco had told her. And now her body was telling her that it wanted Dracco's child.

Somewhere outside the warmth of the bed, beyond the sunlight of the bedroom, lay certain sharply informed realities, but Imogen was in no mood to acknowledge them. What did they matter now? she taunted in silent mental recklessness. What, after last night, could matter more than what she and Dracco had shared? What she had discovered?

The love he had denied her as a girl had been there for her last night. She was sure of it.

The muslin voile curtains moved in the breeze, throwing small shadows across the room that were as ephemeral and as easily despatched as her unwanted doubts.

She loved Dracco. She couldn't not love him and have shared with him, as she had done yesterday, that deepest and most intimate sense of herself. And he surely could not have touched her, aroused her, savoured and satisfied her in the way that he had if he had not cared about her? Loved her in return?

Love. It was such a small word to cover such an infinity of emotion. Did she even truthfully know what it was? She had gone from loving Dracco to hating him, and then last night… Imogen took a deep breath, willing herself to think logically and realistically, but it was no use. Every time she tried to do so all she could see was Dracco's face, all she could feel was his touch, all she could hear was the immeasurably sweet sound of his breathing.

She was twenty-two and a woman, she reminded herself fiercely, and, even though physically she might have been a virgin, she was mature enough to know that sex, however good it might be, wasn't love.

Her heart refused to acknowledge such unworthy thoughts. What she and Dracco had shared had gone way beyond mere sex. It wasn't just one another's bodies they had touched; they had touched one another's hearts, one another's souls. Whatever had happened to them individually in their lives before last night no longer mattered. Her whole body was quivering, singing in the sweet, intoxicating aftermath of love. All she really wanted was to be with Dracco! To drink in the reality of him, breathe in the scent of him.

Imogen smiled ruefully at her own giddiness. She and Dracco needed to talk, to face one another and their shared past.

She took another deep breath. Surely in the light of what had already happened between them they were both adult enough to discuss everything? Their future and their past?

It was time to get up, for her to face the day—and Dracco.

* * *

Her foot poised on the topmost stair, Imogen paused and looked down through the banister into the hallway towards the closed door to what had once been her father's study and was now her husband's. Her husband, Dracco! The melting, delicious warmth just thinking such a thought gave her was a revelation. Dracco. Her husband. The father of her child…their child. A sensation not unlike the delicate touch of a skilled musician on a treasured instrument trembled across her skin.

Suddenly she couldn't wait to see him, to be with him, to reach up and pull that dark head down toward her, to feel those male lips caressing hers.

Light-heartedly she quickened her footsteps.

The study door was closed and Imogen paused outside it, suddenly feeling slightly nervous. Her senses felt preternaturally heightened; she could almost smell and taste the dust motes dancing on the sun-warmed air. The enormity of the moment and what it might portend made her heart beat unsteadily. On the other side of that door lay not just Dracco, but also her future. Their future, and potentially the future of their child.

Instinctively she touched her stomach. It was too soon to know if yesterday…

She gave a small gasp as the study door opened. Dracco was standing within the opening watching her, frowning at her. Her own forehead automatically started to mimic the expression she could see on his, although, whilst his frown was one of impatience and distance, hers was one of questioning concern.

'Imo.'

Even the way he said her name had a certain harshness

about it, Imogen recognised as her glance slid from his face to his body. He was wearing a formidably businesslike dark suit, the jacket unfastened over a crisp white shirt, and as she watched him he shot back his cuff to look at his watch.

One did not need to be an expert at interpreting body language to recognise his impatience.

'You look as though you're very busy. I had hoped that we might be able to talk,' she began.

'Talk? What about?'

It was not a promising start, Imogen acknowledged, but she was not a teenager gazing star-struck at an idol any more. She and Dracco were equals now.

'About us, and last night,' she responded calmly.

Imogen was proud of the way she managed to keep her gaze steady under the pressure of the look Dracco gave her.

'Last night?'

If anything his voice had become even more curt, carrying an edge to it that warned Imogen she was trespassing on a no-go area. But, as Imogen had discovered in the years she had been away, she possessed her own brand of strength and courage, and the issue that lay between them was not one she was going to allow to be ignored.

Moving closer to him, she reiterated softly, 'Yes, Dracco, last night. You do remember last night, don't you?' As she spoke the gentle mockery in her voice gave way to a soft liquid tenderness that shone in her eyes and curled her mouth. 'Last night, when you made love to me. You do remember that, don't you?' she teased.

'What I remember is that we had sex.'

The brutality of the cold words ripped into the shining delicate warmth of Imogen's hopes and dreams.

Now it was her turn to repeat Dracco's words.

'Sex.' She could hear the stammering anxiety in her voice, the desire to be reassured, but Dracco was already turning away from her, looking irritably towards the front door, as though he couldn't wait to escape.

'Dracco,' she protested, and she could hear the pain trembling through her voice. 'It wasn't just sex. It was...'

Helpless in the face of his remoteness, she couldn't bring herself to say the word 'love', to expose it and herself to the savage pain of his contemptuous dismissal. Instead her voice trailed away on an unsteady protest that held echoes of her childhood insecurity as she told him, 'It was more than that.'

'It was sex, Imo,' Dracco overrode her tersely. His head was turned away from her but she could see his profile, see the bleak downward turn of his mouth, the grimness in his expression, which warned her that he wanted the conversation brought to an end.

But there was a stubbornness in her that refused to allow her to let go, and, as though he sensed it, she heard him draw in his breath in open exasperation before he turned fully towards her. His gaze, clinical, cold, rejecting, swept her from head to toe.

'Sex, that's all,' he repeated. 'No more and no less.'

All the fiery passion that was so much a part of her nature rose up inside Imogen.

What she had felt with him, for him, last night was too important to be swept aside. She believed in her feelings and her instincts, even if Dracco didn't, and she was prepared to fight and fight hard if she had to to have them recognised.

'I'm twenty-two years old, Dracco; I've been independent for the last four years. You might remember me as a naïve teenager, but the woman you held in your arms last night, the woman you made love with—'

'Was a naïve virgin,' Dracco cut across her impassioned speech. He was watching her with almost clinical detachment to see how she reacted, how she recovered from the cutting edge of his blow. 'It's true that I do remember you as a child, Imogen. A very immature and romantic young teenager, who idealised the physical relationship between men and women, and who could only allow it into her life wrapped in the pretty packaging of "love". You claim to be mature. But a mature woman would never have clung to her virginity the way you have to yours.'

The cruelty of his clinical dissection of her took Imogen's breath away. It was as though he was determined to strip every last bit of emotion from what they had shared and turn it into something cold and meaningless.

'Psychologically for you,' he continued ruthlessly, 'the mere fact that you have had sex with me—and enjoyed it—means that you have to convince yourself that the physical arousal and desire you felt had to be the product of "love". Loving someone, Imo, means knowing them, accepting them, valuing them as they are. You and I do not...'

Imogen was not prepared to listen to any more. Boldly she stepped up to him; so close to him in fact that she was virtually touching him. As she put her hand on his arm she felt his muscles lock against her touch.

'Imo, I've got an appointment I have to keep, and I'm already dangerously close to being late for it.'

Willing him to allow her through the barriers he had thrown up against her, Imogen leaned into him, whispering, 'Dracco, please… Last night must have meant something to you. I—'

'It meant a great deal.' Imogen felt tears begin to sting her eyes. But her relief was short-lived.

Instead of reassuring her as she longed for him to do, Dracco told her crisply, 'It meant that, if we are lucky, nine months from now we shall have a child—I shall have a son or daughter who carries your father's blood, which is, after all, what this is about.'

He couldn't have made it any plainer to her that she meant nothing to him, Imogen recognised, as he sidestepped her.

Her vision blurred as she stared towards the stairs she had come down less than half an hour ago, her hopes so high, her belief so sure!

Dracco had reached the front door.

Somehow she managed to make herself turn towards him. 'And if…if we aren't lucky?' she challenged him desperately.

There was a small pause before he told her quietly, 'Then in that case we shall just have to try again until we are.'

As he opened the door and walked through it Imogen felt a shudder tear through her body as though it and she were being ripped apart. How could she endure that? The cold lovelessness of the act of sex with a man who did not love her but whom she…

She didn't cry. She couldn't! The pain was like a wound inflicted so deep within her body that it destroyed internally without any outward evidence of the injury.

Dracco got down the drive and as far as the main road without giving in to his emotions, but once there he recognised that, feeling as he did right now, he was a danger to himself and to others.

Cursing sharply beneath his breath, he pulled off the road and stopped his car.

He had lied to Imo about the urgency of his appointment. He was on his way to see David Bryant to sign the new will he had had the other man draw up.

'You want to make Imogen and any child she might conceive the main beneficiaries of your estate?' David had commented when Dracco informed him of his wishes. 'We're talking about a very large inheritance, Dracco. You say you want Imogen to have full control of it?' He had paused uncertainly. 'It is customary where such a large amount is concerned to appoint trustees or set up a trust fund.'

'There is no one I trust more than Imogen,' Dracco had responded firmly.

Imogen would never know just what last night had done to him, the sheer unbearable immensity of the guilt and remorse it had brought him—and the pleasure! So much pleasure that it was impossible to quantify it. How could he measure something that had been so longed and hungered for? How could he estimate the breadth and depth of how he had felt when after a virtually sleepless night he had leaned over in the first minutes of the new day to look down into her sleeping face?

Even in her sleep she had been smiling, her lips curved in soft, sensuous warmth. The tears of release and fulfilment she had cried in his arms had gone, but their salty trail had lain gently crystallised on her skin. Beneath the bedclothes she'd been naked, and the temptation to run his hand possessively down her body from the top of her head right the way to her toes, just for the luxurious pleasure of knowing she was there, had almost overwhelmed him.

He knew he had given her pleasure—would have known it even if she had not cried it out to him in a voice of shocked, delighted wonder—simply from the way her body had responded to him, fitted itself around him, accepted and embraced his touch upon it and within it.

But he had always known that there would be pleasure between them; had known it from the moment he had looked beyond the shy awkwardness of the girl she'd been and seen the woman she would become. She had desired him then with all the innocent hunger of a young girl's awakening sexuality and he had known it, and known too that he was equally drawn by longing to her as she was to him. The only difference had been that he'd been an adult and she had not. An adult male with an adult male's needs for a mate, a woman.

Dracco closed his eyes and breathed in, filling his lungs.

What he had told her about wanting her father's blood to run in the veins of his own child had been true, but it was only a small part of the truth.

John Atkins had been an astute and loving father. He had seen as clearly as Dracco had himself the growing intensity of Imogen's youthful crush on Dracco.

'She imagines herself in love with you,' John had told him in a no-holds-barred man-to-man conversation he had instituted shortly before Imogen's sixteenth birthday.

'I know,' Dracco had concurred. 'I love her, John,' he had told his friend and mentor rawly, 'and I know too that she is far too young as yet—'

'Dracco,' John Atkins had interrupted him immediately, 'I don't dispute your feelings, but, as Imogen's father, I would ask you to give me your word that you will allow her to have time to grow up and experience life before you tell her of your love. If you love her you'll understand why I'm asking you this.'

And of course Dracco had, even though the thought of having to stand to one side and watch whilst the girl he loved grew into womanhood with someone else had torn him apart.

'If you and Imogen should eventually become a couple,' John Atkins had continued emotionally, 'and I can promise you that there is nothing that would give me more pleasure, Dracco, it has to be as two equals, adults, not now whilst Imogen, for all she thinks she is passionately in love with you, is still little more than a child. I know how hard what I'm asking of you is going to be but, for Imogen's own sake and for the sake of the love I hope you may one day share, will you promise to say nothing of your feelings to her until she is twenty-one?'

Twenty-one. Five years! But Dracco had known why John was demanding such a promise from him, and he had given it. Had Imogen been his daughter he would have done exactly the same thing.

He had told himself after her father's death that he owed it to his friend and mentor to protect his only daughter, if necessary against himself, but then circumstances had left him with no choice other than to marry Imogen, for her own sake.

How he had agonised over that decision, ultimately seeking the advice of Henry Fairburn, John's solicitor and oldest friend.

He had told himself that he would not break his word to John, that he would somehow find the strength to make sure that his marriage to Imogen was in name only and that she knew nothing of his feelings for her.

But then as they'd left the church she had asked him if there was someone he loved, and he had known that she knew the truth, had seen in her eyes that she already knew the answer to her own question. Her reaction to it had made it plain how she felt.

After all, there was no more obvious a way of stating that someone's love was not wanted than to run away from them.

Lisa had taunted him about it, saying that he should have left Imogen to play teenage sex games with someone of her own age, claiming that the thought of having sex with a real live man had probably terrified her.

'A real man needs a real woman, Dracco,' she had told him, her hand on his arm, stroking it suggestively. He had shrugged her off, barely able to conceal either his dislike or his pain at losing Imogen.

Out of guilt and remorse and pain he had managed to

stop himself from going after Imogen and bringing her back.

How could he possibly have claimed to love her and then forced her to accept that love when she didn't want it?

And then David Bryant had told him about the letter he had received from her, and, almost as though he was watching himself from a distance, a part of Dracco had looked on in grim contempt whilst he set about making plans to…

To what? Couldn't he even admit to himself what he had done? Well, perhaps it was time he did. He had manoeuvred and manipulated Imogen into coming back to him. And the result had far exceeded even the most fevered scenarios conjured up by the long lonely nights of wanting her.

To hear that note of wonderment in her voice earlier when she had talked about last night, about them 'making love', had made him want to take hold of her right there and show her that last night had been a mere fraction of what they could share together. But what he wanted from her was a lot more than the orgasm-induced emotion of physical satisfaction. What he wanted was her love, a love that matched his own; a love that went way beyond the giving and taking of pleasure in bed. Yes, it was satisfying to know that physically Imo wanted him, but it was a bitter, tainted pleasure. It was her love he wanted, not her body, and how the hell could he ever win that after what he had done?

Even now Dracco found it hard to explain to himself why he had overreacted so uncharacteristically when Imogen had assumed that he wanted a divorce.

Yes, of course he wanted her to have his child, and, yes, he very much wanted to share a blood tie with the man who had meant so much to him, but to use that as an excuse to force Imo to consummate their marriage… There was no acceptable explanation for what he had done.

Dracco opened his eyes. He had kept track of Imogen all the time they had been apart, knowing that it was what her father would have expected him to do.

He had never for one moment intended… But somehow things had got out of hand; and he had found it far harder to control his feelings than he had expected. The reality of dealing with a fully grown woman and not a girl had brought it home to him how dangerously vulnerable he actually was.

He had tried to keep as much physical distance between them as he could, working away from home, sleeping downstairs in the study. But last night all those plans had been crushed out of existence, along with his self-control. Last night he had done the very thing he had promised himself he would never, ever do under any circumstances.

And now Imo was telling him that she loved him. Not because she did—dammit—but because he was her first lover, her only lover. For a woman as idealistic as Imogen, that meant she could not allow herself the physical pleasure they had shared without convincing herself that she must love him. But she hadn't loved him when she had run away from him on the day of their marriage.

He had seen the hurt in her eyes when she had turned away in the hallway just now, and he had ached to take her in his arms and tell her just how he felt about her, just what she did to him, had always done to him.

Right now he didn't know which was causing him the greater pain—his love for her or his guilt.

Dracco closed his eyes again. He had no idea how long he had been sitting here in his car, and neither did he care. He was back in the study of the house he had just left, Imo's father's study. It was the morning of Imo's seventeenth birthday, the morning she had run downstairs to him and begged him shyly for a birthday kiss, when he had known that he had to plead with his mentor and friend to release him from his promise.

'Yes, I know how hard it is, Dracco,' John Atkins had accepted gently when Dracco had finished his terse little speech. 'But Imogen is only seventeen.'

'Seventeen going on a thousand,' Dracco had groaned. 'She looks at me sometimes with all the knowledge of every woman that ever lived in her eyes, and then at other times…' He had paused and shaken his head. 'At other times she looks at me with the unknowing innocence of a child.'

'And it is the innocence and the future of that child I would ask you to protect and respect, Dracco,' Imogen's father had responded gently, getting to his feet and coming to Dracco's side, placing his hand on Dracco's arm in a benign, almost fatherly gesture.

He had paused before continuing in a sterner voice, 'If you love her you will want her to give you her love as a woman, not take from her the naïve love of a child.'

His words had hit home, and Dracco had acknowledged their truth.

'Nothing will ever change the way I feel about her,'

he had told the older man fiercely. 'But for her sake I will do as you ask, and I will wait.'

'It is nearly as hard for me as it for you, Dracco,' Imogen's father had told him gently. 'When I said I love you as a son that is exactly what I meant, and I can think of no greater pleasure than having you marry my daughter unless it is that of holding your children. But Imo is far too young yet to be burdened by a man's love. She needs time and space to grow up properly.'

Dracco hated himself for what he had done last night. He felt corrupted by his own emotions, his love, his desire, the constant, aching need for Imogen that had flared into a fiercely unstoppable conflagration the moment he had touched her.

He could feel it still now, knew he would feel it forever, just as he would love her forever.

It was over an hour since he had stopped his car. Reaching for his mobile, Dracco put a call through to David Bryant to explain that he was going to be late for their meeting.

Tugging viciously at the nettles growing in amongst the roses she could remember her mother planting, Imogen muttered an angry protest as she felt them stinging her through the thickness of the gardening gloves she had found in the old-fashioned potting shed.

Dracco's rejection of her love and the scorn with which he had reacted to it and to her, instead of making her question the validity of her feelings had somehow had totally the opposite effect and brought out in her a passionate strength she had not guessed she possessed.

How dared he try to tell her that she did not know

what love was? She tugged furiously on another nettle, giving a small sound of triumph as she threw it into the wheelbarrow without getting stung.

How dared he imply that she was some kind of naïve ninny who thought that just because she had sex with a man she must be in love with him?

Another nettle joined its fellows.

And as for his comments about her virginity... Well, it just so happened that the reason she had not...that she was still...had been still...had nothing to do with naïveté or timidity; it was simply that she had never met a man she had wanted enough.

Imogen yelped in pain as her momentary loss of concentration, whilst she battled against the dangerous images her brain was sending, resulted in a sharp reminder that nettles, carelessly handled, could and did sting.

'Ouch,' she protested out loud, as she inspected the swiftly lifting rash on the palm of her hand.

Like Dracco, it had caught her off guard and the result was pain. Well, this time at least she could retaliate, she decided grimly as she bent towards the offending weed and very determinedly removed it from the soil.

'Now see how you like that!' she told the nettle triumphantly.

'Excuse me.'

The sound of a hesitant male voice behind her caused her to spin round, her face pink with confusion at being caught conversing with the vegetation.

'It stung me,' she said rather lamely to the young man who was standing several feet away from her.

'My wife hates nettles,' he responded easily. 'Her

brothers hid her doll in a nettle patch when she was a little girl.'

'Oh, how unkind of them.'

'Well, I suspect she might have deserved it,' he told her, his voice ruefully candid. 'She had buried all their toy soldiers in a pile of builders' sand. The builder wasn't too pleased when it ruined his concrete. Her excuse was that they had been overwhelmed by a sandstorm in the desert.

'I was looking for Dracco,' he went on. 'I rang the bell but no one answered and then I saw you here in the garden. You must be his wife.'

'Yes, yes, I am,' Imogen responded. Who was this young man, and how did he know that Dracco was married?

As though he guessed what she was thinking, her unexpected visitor quickly explained, 'I'm Robert Bates—I work for Dracco. He left a message at the office, saying that…that he had got married, and asking me to bring him some papers he wanted.'

He was looking rather pleased with his deductive powers, and Imogen couldn't resist gently teasing him.

'And because of that you assumed that I must be Dracco's wife?'

'Not just because of that,' she was told sturdily. 'He has a photograph of you on his desk, and I recognised you from it straight away. Your father started the business, didn't he? Dracco told me about him.'

Now Imogen was surprised. Dracco had a photograph of her? She remembered that her father had had one taken on her seventeenth birthday; presumably Dracco must have inherited it. However, before she could reply her visitor was saying something she found even more surprising.

'I know that your father started the business, but Dracco is the one who made it the success it is today.' As he spoke Imogen could hear the admiration and respect in the younger man's voice. 'I couldn't believe my luck when he took me on. I didn't have the qualifications or the background.' He flushed a little whilst Imogen watched him in silence. 'I certainly didn't deserve the faith he's shown in me. The night we met I was sitting in a bar, full of self-pity and drinking myself into oblivion. Natasha, my wife now but my girlfriend as she was then, had just told me that her parents had threatened her that if she married me they were going to stop her trust fund.

'We met at university and I knew straight away that she was the one for me, and she said she felt the same, but what I didn't know then was that Natasha's family had money—and ambitions.' His voice grew slightly bitter. 'And those ambitions did not include a son-in-law with no family connections, no money and no prospects. Oh, Tasha said that it didn't matter, but of course it did. I couldn't give her the kind of life she'd grown up with, the kind of future she deserved; I couldn't even get a job. And then I met Dracco.

'He gave me a job, and time off so that I could get my Masters in business studies; he let me and Tasha live rent-free in a flat above the offices. He even went to see Tasha's parents, and God knows what he said to them but…' He broke off and gave Imogen an embarrassed look. 'I don't know why I'm telling you all this. After all, you already know exactly what kind of man Dracco is—you're married to him.'

He paused and then added hesitantly, 'Once when I asked him why he had helped me he said it was because I reminded him of what he himself had once been, and of everything that your father had done for him. He said that he wanted to pass on the good deed your father had done, to honour his memory and to show his gratitude for it. He said that your father had taught him the value of true generosity of spirit and the importance of self-respect.'

Imogen felt sharp tears sting her eyes in the small silence that followed. When she was sure she had full control of herself she offered, 'I'll give Dracco the papers if you want to leave them with me. But first let's go up to the house. I'm ready for a cup of tea; would you like one?'

'No, I'd better not. I promised Tasha I'd be home early. It's our wedding anniversary today, and her parents are taking us out to dinner!'

After her unexpected visitor had driven away Imogen couldn't help thinking about what he had said to her.

She had come out into the garden after Dracco's departure, ready to hate him all over again, but now she had been shown a compassionate side of him that made her feel uncertain.

Her hand felt acutely painful where the nettles had stung her. She had always been sensitive to their sting and an unpleasant tingling numbness now accompanied the raised rash, swelling the palm of her hand and her fingers.

She massaged it absently, thinking about her father.

She had always known how much he had thought of Dracco, and he had been held in high esteem by his peers for his shrewd judgement. She wished that he were here now for her to turn to.

Dracco still hadn't come back. And when he did... She quickly calculated how long it might be before she would know if she was pregnant.

And if she wasn't? Her face burned with mortified colour as she recognised that the bumping of her heart against her ribs at the thought of a repetition of the previous night was quite definitely not caused by dread or revulsion. Far from it. But Dracco did not love her and, according to him, she could not love him.

Who had he been thinking of whilst he touched her body, whilst he aroused it, entered it, possessed and filled it with the gift of immortality?

Imogen willed the acid sting of the tears burning her eyes not to fall.

As a child she had cried over her loss of her father's love to Lisa. As a woman there was no way she was going to cry over the loss of Dracco's love to her stepmother. No way at all!

Imogen sighed as she heard someone pressing impatiently and repeatedly on the front doorbell. Today was quite obviously her day for visitors.

Running lightly downstairs, she pulled open the front door, to reveal the features of her uninvited guest.

'Lisa!' It was impossible for Imogen to keep the shock out of her voice.

Her stepmother was wearing a pair of white Capri pants, her face and body tanned from her Caribbean holiday. Glaring at Imogen, she stepped into the hallway without waiting for an invitation and demanded sharply, 'Where's Dracco? I need to speak to him. Is he in the study?' She was walking towards the door before Imogen could stop her.

'No, he isn't,' Imogen told her as calmly as she could.

Seeing her stepmother here in the house which her presence had made so unhappy would have been bad enough, but knowing what Imogen now knew made that pain a thousand times worse.

'Then where is he?' Lisa was asking her angrily.

'He's out on business,' Imogen told her reluctantly. She would have preferred not to have to answer her at all. She would have preferred, in fact, to have enough belief in Dracco's support to insist that Lisa leave the house immediately.

'You mean he's sleeping at the apartment in London because he can't bear to have to sleep here with you?' Lisa taunted aggressively. 'It's a pity you were always so pathetically antagonistic towards me, Imogen. Had you not been you might have learned one or two things of value. Such as the fact that there is nothing that a man abhors more than a woman who doesn't have the pride to accept it when he makes it obvious he doesn't want her. And Dracco doesn't want you, Imogen. He never has wanted you. On the other hand, of course, he did want the business. And who can blame him? I certainly don't. Miranda warned me that you had come crawling back to him. Somehow I wasn't totally surprised. But it won't do you any good.'

Imogen had heard enough. She wasn't a shy, grieving teenager any more, who instinctively believed she had to be polite to grown-ups no matter how offensive and rude they were to her. It was high time that Lisa had a taste of her own medicine and Imogen was in just the mood to hand it out to her! After all, what had she got to lose? Dracco had already told her that he didn't love her. That they had only had sex!

If in punishing Lisa she punished Dracco as well, so much the better. He deserved it—they both did! Imogen couldn't remember ever feeling so furiously, gloriously angry!

She was a woman betrayed, a woman scorned, and those who had done the betraying and the scorning had just better watch out. They were going to find out that she could give as good as she got!

'As a matter of fact, it was Dracco who insisted on giving our marriage a second chance, not me,' she told Lisa with pseudo-sweetness. If she hadn't been enjoying herself so much she might almost have been shocked by the savage sense of satisfaction it gave her to say the words that were responsible for the brief look of fury she saw in Lisa's eyes. 'And it isn't just my share of the business he wants, Lisa,' she continued recklessly, only distantly aware of just how dangerous the surge of euphoria sweeping her up into its enticing embrace might be.

'Well, it can't possibly be your body!' Lisa retaliated nastily. 'If it was he'd be here with you now.'

'Perhaps I should leave it to him to tell you just what he wants from our marriage,' Imogen suggested serenely. She was almost enjoying the effect her words were having on her stepmother, who was staring at her as though she was seeing her properly for the first time. 'Unless, of course, he has already told you?'

Lisa gave a dismissive shrug. 'Dracco and I don't discuss you, Imogen, we have far more important things to talk about.'

Imogen could feel her self-control cracking as the euphoria left her as suddenly as it had swept her up, leaving in its wake a wash of anguished pain. 'Yes,' she agreed bitterly. 'Such as the way the pair of you deceived my father.'

She could see from the smirk the other woman was giving that she had allowed her emotions to betray her.

'You're making assumptions, accusations that you simply can't prove, Imogen.'

'I don't have to prove them,' Imogen retorted. 'Both you and Dracco have already shown me how true they are. Your affair—'

'Dracco told you we had an affair?' Lisa stopped her. For some reason she was frowning, as though she didn't believe what Imogen was telling her. But then unexpectedly she smiled, as though she was actually pleased to be revealed as a woman who had broken her marriage vows.

'He didn't need to tell me. You did that…on my wedding day,' Imogen reminded her grimly.

Lisa's smile widened. 'Yes, so I did. Poor little Imogen; you were so naïve, so stupid… Umm… Well, if Dracco is at the office I suppose I'd better go and see him there. I'm sure he'll appreciate the privacy for our reunion,' she purred tauntingly. 'It's been almost a month since he last saw me, and a month for a man of

Dracco's sexual appetite is a very long time. Don't expect him home too soon, will you, Mrs Barrington?'

She was walking through the door before Imogen could frame any kind of suitably cutting retort.

So it was true. Dracco was still seeing Lisa. He still loved her.

She wasn't going to cry, Imogen told herself with fierce pride. She wasn't!

CHAPTER SEVEN

'IMO, are you all right?'

'I'm fine, thank you,' Imogen responded, her voice as carefully devoid of any emotion as she could make it.

'Then why aren't you eating your dinner?' Dracco demanded sharply.

They had been living together as man and wife for just over a month, and Imogen had used the vast oasis of time Dracco's absences in London on business gave her. He had put his bank account at her disposal to set about restoring and refurbishing the house—it helped to keep her surface busy, during the day at least. At night, those long, lonely, aching nights when her thoughts and feelings couldn't be kept at bay, she felt as though she had entered a painful form of purgatory.

Not once since she had called at the house demanding to see him had he mentioned Lisa, and Imogen was stubbornly, bitterly determined not to be the one to bring up her name. Because she was afraid that if she did she would not be able to conceal what she really felt?

Lisa's cruel taunts had hit home. Had Dracco told Lisa just what he wanted from their marriage? There was no way Imogen could have borne to know that the man she loved was contemplating having a child with another woman, even a woman he did not love, but then Lisa had never been in the least bit maternal.

'Because I'm not hungry.' Imogen answered Dracco's

question coolly, lifting her gaze to meet his down the length of the pretty table she had seen in an antique shop and bought for a sum that had given her a vicious slam of guilt that was only slightly appeased by the pleasure it gave her to run her fingertips over the old satiny polished, wood.

A little to her own surprise, she had slipped back into life here in their small market town with unexpected ease. It was true that she had not made any close friends in Rio for her to miss. Her past had made it difficult for her to talk openly with her co-workers, and Dracco's rejection of her had left painful scars that had damaged her self-confidence.

She still thought about Rio, of course, and the children. After all, it was because of her determination to help them that she was trapped in this unbearable nightmare situation. One day she would go back, but right now there were issues closer to hand that were absorbing her time and attention!

'What is it, Dracco?' she challenged him. 'Were you hoping I was going to say I wasn't eating it because I felt sick? Because I'm pregnant?' She shook her head and gave him an unkind smile. 'I'm sorry to disappoint you, but I'm afraid that I'm not. Poor you, you're going to have to force yourself to have sex with me all over again.' She gave a small, brittle laugh as fragile as the crystal in the wine glasses they were drinking out of.

She scarcely recognised herself in the embittered woman she felt she was becoming. Was this what sex did to you when it was denied to you? When you were given a taste of what it could be and then not allowed to taste it again?

Imogen had no way of knowing; after all, as Dracco had said himself, what did she know about sex? She had been a naïve virgin when he had taken her to bed, a fool who confused sex with love and who believed that love mattered.

'Perhaps we should be more scientific and work out exactly when there is the optimum chance of me conceiving. After all, neither of us wants to have sex unnecessarily.' Somehow she managed to produce a sweetly disdainful little smile as she made this suggestion.

'You're lying to me, Imo!'

For a moment she was so caught off guard that she looked at him in shock. He was only guessing. He couldn't possibly know… She wasn't even properly sure herself… That unfamiliar bout of dizziness and the fact that she could not bear her normal cup of strong coffee in the morning was all the evidence she had to go on as yet.

'You want sex, and right now you want it so badly that I could take you right here, and, believe me, I'm sorely tempted to do just that, if only to prove it to you.'

Imogen went limp with relief. He didn't know. He hadn't meant what she had thought he meant at all. And then the reality of what he was saying pierced the blanket of her relief in tiny shocking darts of electric expectancy.

'You're wrong. I don't want you.'

What on earth was she doing, pushing him to the point where he would have no choice but to…?

Imogen gave a small gasp as Dracco got up from his seat and started to walk purposefully towards her.

'I've warned you before about challenging me, Imo,' he reminded her.

He had reached her now and pulled her easily to her feet and up against his body, holding her there as he looked down into her eyes, his mouth curling with insolence whilst his gaze lingered with deliberate intent on her mouth and then her throat, where her pulse was beating frantically fast, before dropping to her breasts.

It had been a hot day and she was wearing a thin top, against which her nipples had suddenly started to push with impatient eagerness.

Very carefully Dracco flattened the fabric against one of them, studying the openly erect outline in a way that made the heat flaming her face nothing to the heat burning inside her body.

'But then, this is exactly what you wanted me to do, isn't it?' he asked her softly.

Her denial never got beyond her throat, because suddenly Dracco was covering her mouth with his, kissing her with a fierce, smothering passion that her own senses leapt to meet.

It was almost as though they were fighting a battle that each was determined to win, anger searing and sizzling through both of them.

As his mouth possessed hers Imogen made an attempt to bite at it, forestalled by the fierce thrust of his tongue between her parted lips. She could feel its smooth roughness against the edge of her teeth and then its hot, dominating slide against her own tongue.

Something inside her started to melt. She gave a keening moan, her fingers curling into the thin cotton shirt he was wearing. As though she had crushed a flower in her fingers, she could smell the hot scent of him her grip had released. It dizzied her, sending a wave of longing melting through her, a slow, sweet melt of butter-soft pleasure.

'Dracco!'

She felt his mouth take his name from her as her lips formed it; knew he had absorbed and recognised the need that pierced her with such shocking sweetness.

Behind her closed eyelids she could see his naked body already, remember it in intimate and erotic detail, every bone, every muscle, every heart-wrenchingly perfect inch of him.

'I want you so much.'

The words were drawn from her as painfully as tears. She was powerless to suppress them and even more powerless to suppress her love for him. But it wasn't love. Dracco had told her that. It was just sex!

Her whole body shuddered.

Did Lisa make him react like this? Did he make her want him like this?

The savagery of her feelings lacerated her pride, but somehow she couldn't withstand the pressure of her need.

'Take me to bed, Dracco,' she urged him.

Because she wanted him or because she wanted to prove to herself that she was woman enough to overpower his resistance? That what Lisa had done she too could do?

She felt him hesitate.

'You were the one who wanted this,' she reminded him. 'You're the one who wants me to have your child.'

She knew, of course, that when she returned to sanity,

when the madness of her longing and misery left her, she would despise herself for using such a weapon, for demeaning herself. But right now, what did such things matter? Right now she wanted him so much…too much.

This time it was different. This time she was anticipating every touch, every sensation, savagely hungry for him, her body rising up to meet him and demanding more. More!

But then abruptly, like someone who had fed themselves on rich confectionery, she suddenly felt nauseated by what she was doing, appalled and disgusted by her own greed and lack of self-control.

This was sex, she reminded herself. Sex, not love. Was she really so lacking in self-control, in self-respect, that she could be satisfied with a physical act given without any kind of emotional grace?

'What is it?'

She could feel Dracco's hands holding her stiffening body as he leaned over her in the summer darkness.

'I've changed my mind.'

She could feel the sharpness of his indrawn breath.

'Am I allowed to ask why?'

She could hear the tension underlying the outwardly silky words.

'You wouldn't understand.' Any minute now she was going to cry. Defensively she turned her head away from him.

'Try me.'

Was it her imagination or was his voice softer, gentler? His hands on her arms certainly were. She could feel him rubbing her skin, soothing it, stroking it as though in some way he was trying to reassure and comfort her. A touch could say so much more than words. A touch couldn't lie…could it? Or was it more that her lack of experience was making her read too much into it?

She felt drained, defeated, overwhelmed by her emotions.

'I don't want it to be just sex between us, Dracco.'

There was a long silence whilst she waited for him to answer, during which Imogen asked herself furiously why on earth she had made such an admission.

'No? Then what do you want it to be?'

His hands were on her shoulders now, cupping them, working up delicately towards her throat, gently massaging away her tension.

Imogen gave a small gasp as she felt the tiny quivers of sensation darting over her skin. The pulse at the base of her throat had started to beat fast again. Dracco placed his thumb on it, measuring it, and then lifted his hand to her lips, rubbing against her bottom lip very slowly.

'Tell me, Imogen,' he demanded huskily, his voice a soft, sensual enticement. 'What is it you want from me?'

Her whole body was trembling now. It was those two little words 'from me' that had done it.

'I want you, Dracco!' she told him helplessly. 'I want you.'

And then she was reaching for his mouth with her own, devouring it with tiny, longing-filled little kisses interspersed with soft, whispery moans.

It wasn't the way it had been before. It was sharper, sweeter, deeper, with her not merely responding but actively drawing her own response from him! Touching him with fingers that trembled slightly and then grew more confident as she saw the naked agony of wanting delineating every aspect of his expression. He wanted her touch, needed it, yearned for it so much that he was prepared to walk across burning coals to get to it and her. It gave Imogen a wave of shockingly savage pleasure to see it.

She rode that pleasure like a surfer, telling herself that she was the one controlling it and Dracco, until suddenly it crested, splintering her into a thousand diamond darts of tormentingly hot need which only the sure thrust of Dracco's body within her own could satisfy.

Only when it was over and she was sure that Dracco was asleep did she allow herself to cry, to grieve for what Dracco had not given her—his love.

It didn't matter what Dracco said, what male logic he tried to superimpose on her feelings to validate his own lack of love for her and force an emotional distance between them, Imogen knew she loved him. She didn't want to and it galled and lacerated her sensitive pride to know that she did.

She had lost count of the time she had wasted trying to rationalise her emotions, trying to list mentally all the reasons she had for not loving him. Her heart just wasn't prepared to listen to them. Not even when she tormented it with the strongest antidote of all—not even when she reminded it about Lisa!

Imogen hesitated as she stopped her car outside the house, next to Dracco's. He had told her only the previous evening that he intended to work as much as he could in future from home.

'With modern technology I don't really need a London base any more, and, besides…' He had glanced with deliberate emphasis at her stomach as he spoke. Imogen had felt a now familiar fluttering of guilty panic invade her body.

Sometimes it was almost as though he already knew and he was deliberately directing the conversation down an avenue that would give her no choice but to tell him of her own growing conviction that she had conceived their child.

But she didn't want to do so. Not yet. And, anyway, she had nothing official to go on. Only her own awed belief that she was carrying a new life. She could quite easily have found out one way or the other, but she didn't want to do so, and she didn't want to question just why not either.

Was it because she wanted to punish him? Or was it because a part of her hoped that his desire to father their child would keep him close to her and away from Lisa?

She was beginning to hate what her love for him was making her do, the kind of woman it was turning her into. What had happened to her moral beliefs, her pride?

They were having a truly golden summer weather-wise, and in their local town this morning she had bumped into a friend from her schooldays. They had had coffee together, exchanging recent histories. Lulu, her friend, had been living with her partner since they had left university. She had recently been headhunted for a job, which would mean her relocating to New York.

'I envy you,' she had confessed to Imogen. 'You've done things the right way around, explored the world and then settled down. I can't bear the thought of losing Mac, but I want to do something with my life. I want to see something of the world, to explore it and my own talents.'

'Won't Mac go with you?' Imogen had asked her sympathetically.

'Not a chance,' Lulu had told her ruefully. 'He wants us to get married, have babies.' She had pulled a wry face. 'I've got three brothers and five step-siblings, the youngest of whom is still in nappies… Right now the thought of a baby…'

'Do you love him?' Imogen had asked her quietly.

The look Lulu had given her in response to her question had spoken volumes.

'You're right,' Lulu had agreed ruefully. 'I'm just going to have to accustom myself to the thought of frequent transatlantic travel—and finding a good nanny.'

They had parted, agreeing that they must make a regular date to meet up, and Imogen had driven back to the house reflecting on how good it felt to have started to develop a network of supportive friends.

A new interior-design business had opened in the town, and Imogen had arranged for the young women who ran it to call at the house one day so that they could discuss some ideas Imogen had for redecorating.

As she walked through the back door Dracco came into the kitchen. As always when she saw him Imogen's feelings were mixed and very emotional. She loved and wanted him so much, and yet at the same time she dreaded being with him because of the pain it gave her to know that he did not return her feelings.

'I thought we might have lunch out today,' Dracco

announced, casually removing the supermarket bags she was carrying and starting to put away their contents for her.

'I…I thought you were working?' she responded uncertainly.

Dracco paused in the act of opening the fridge door.

'I am, but I can take a couple of hours off. You mentioned that you'd like to do something with the garden; there's a particularly good garden centre with its own design team, a specialist outfit that has an excellent reputation, about ten miles away.'

Imogen chewed on her bottom lip. It was true that she did want to redesign the garden. With the needs of an active toddler to consider, the notion of a safe enclosed play area close to the house quite naturally appealed to her.

She and Dracco hadn't been out together as a couple since the early days of their reunion, nearly two months ago now. She chewed harder on her lip. He was spending more time at home, though.

'There's a very good restaurant where we could have lunch down by the river,' Dracco was saying.

If she was to refuse to go with him he might be tempted to ask Lisa. The sheer savagery of the jealousy that gored her made her catch her breath. What was the matter? She ought to hate and despise him for what he was doing, for what he was, instead of… What she was feeling was totally illogical! But then, when had love ever been anything else?

Helplessly Imogen watched him. She could feel the sheer intensity of her love melting her resistance.

'When were you thinking of leaving?' she asked him.

'Now,' Dracco told her promptly, putting the last of the groceries away and then coming towards her. 'Ready?'

His hand was beneath her elbow, guiding her back towards the door. What was the point of denying herself the opportunity of being with him when she wanted it so much? When she wanted him so much, she acknowledged with a small, sensual shudder of pleasure at his touch.

'No, not a pond.'

Imogen could feel the sharp look Dracco gave her as she shook her head in rejection of the garden designer's suggestion for a water feature in the patio area proposed for the garden.

'But you love the garden's existing formal fish pond,' Dracco reminded her with a small frown.

'Yes, I do,' Imogen agreed. She could feel her face starting to burn self-consciously as both men looked at her, waiting for her to explain her rejection. 'I was thinking that a pond so close to the house might not be a good idea,' she began hesitantly, pausing before continuing, 'Small children can drown so easily and quickly in even a few inches of water.'

The young garden designer gave a small, approving nod.

'Of course. I should have realised. And there are some totally child-safe alternatives that we could discuss—water bubbling over pebbles; that sort of thing.'

As she listened to him Imogen was conscious of Dracco's silence and his concentrated gaze, although he waited until she had thanked the designer for his suggestions and moved out of his earshot before bending his head to murmur speculatively in her ear, 'There isn't anything you want to tell me, is there, Imo?'

'No.' Imogen knew she sounded both defensive and flustered. 'When there is something...anything...to tell you then I will.'

'I'm sure that you will,' Dracco agreed urbanely. 'After all, there's no way you're going to put yourself in the position of having to have sex again with me—unnecessarily—is there? Mmm?'

Imogen gave him a seethingly angry look. How dared he torment her like this, mocking her for her vulnerability to him, for her desire for him?

He had taken to coming to bed later, so late, in fact, that by the time he eventually did so she had fallen into an exhausted sleep.

And she knew why, of course. He didn't want to sleep with her because he really wanted Lisa. How could he be so cruel, so uncaring of her feelings? Surely he must know just how much he was hurting her?

Their lunch, followed by a walk along the river, and then well over an hour here at the garden centre had left her feeling unusually tired. She had noticed increasingly over the last few days a lassitude which tended to overwhelm her during the afternoons, sometimes to such an extent that she had actually fallen asleep. Luckily the hot, sunny spell of weather they were having meant that she could lie in the garden on a sun lounger and doze off to sleep under the pretext of sunbathing.

Now, as they walked back to Dracco's car, Imogen could feel her footsteps lagging, and despite her frantic attempts to do so she couldn't quite manage to smother a sleepy yawn.

Dracco, of course, saw it and stopped in mid-stride to frown down at her and demand, 'Tired?'

'It disturbs my sleep when you come to bed so late,' Imogen parried.

'If that's meant to be a hint that you'd like me to come to bed earlier…?'

'It isn't,' Imogen denied immediately. 'Why should I want you to? I'm not the one who forced this marriage on you, Dracco.'

Before he could retaliate she hurried ahead of him, and then ignored him when he caught up with her just as she reached the car.

A young family of three small children and their father were playing with a ball, and as she watched them Imogen was suddenly reminded of the street children in Rio. Not that these well-fed and obviously very much loved children in front of her were anything like Rio's unwanted orphans, but seeing them made her think about her old life and the people she had shared it with.

Unexpectedly she suddenly ached for the stalwart comfort of Sister Maria's calm wisdom.

Imogen woke up with a start. She had actually gone to bed after their return from the garden centre, claiming not totally untruthfully that she had a headache. Having showered and re-dressed, she headed lethargically for the stairs. Soon now she was going to have to put her suspicions to the test, not that she really had any doubts that she was pregnant, but once that knowledge was 'official' then she was honour-bound to make it known to Dracco.

Normally a couple looked forward to the arrival of a child, especially a wanted child, as an event that would bring them closer together, but in their case Imogen was certain that it would have totally the opposite effect. Once she had given him the child he wanted there would be no room in Dracco's life for her.

Halfway down the stairs, where they turned at a right angle to themselves, there was a small half-landing with a tall, deep window that overlooked the driveway. The stained glass in it had a soft-hued richness which had always delighted Imogen. She stopped automatically to look through it and then froze as she recognised the familiar figure of her stepmother picking her way from her car to the front door on spindly high-heeled sandals.

So far as she knew, Lisa had not visited the house since their confrontation.

Instinctively Imogen stepped back out of sight as Lisa rang the front-doorbell. She heard the study door open and held her breath as she listened to Dracco's strong masculine footsteps and felt the small surge of early-evening air waft into the hallway as he opened the door.

'Lisa.' His voice was expressionless, but in a way that dragged sharp, poisoned nails of anguish across Imogen's heart.

Since Lisa's previous visit to the house Imogen had not confronted the role she knew her stepmother had played and she suspected continued to play in Dracco's life. But her awareness of it shadowed every aspect of their life together. Lying awake on her own in their bed at night she had tormented herself with the knowledge that Dracco was staying away from her because he really wanted to be with Lisa.

She had known exactly why Dracco had not wanted her love, and why he had been so insistent that all they had done together was to have sex, a physical coupling devoid of emotion. He kept his love only for Lisa. And yet, knowing that, she had still wanted him, responded to him, stupidly allowed herself to believe in the impossible fantasy that she, Imogen, had to mean something to him, that he couldn't possibly be with her if she didn't. She had even been so desperate for his love that she had allowed him to mock her for her own helpless desire for him.

Every time he taunted her about it she sensed some deep, hidden, ambivalent feeling behind his words. Because he resented her for taking what should only be given to the woman he loved?

Imogen could feel herself starting to shiver and then to shudder, deep, racking manifestations of her traumatic emotional pain. She could hear Lisa saying with soft seductiveness, 'I knew you'd be expecting me.'

And then the study door was closing, shutting her out, enclosing both of them in their own private world.

If she closed her eyes Imogen could see them in it...could see the way the late-afternoon sun would illuminate dust motes of gold through the long sash windows either side of the traditional fireplace her father had insisted on keeping. The desk, an antique partners' desk at which she could vividly remember both her father and Dracco sitting, working amicably together, was in one corner of the room. Behind it were floor-to-ceiling bookcases. To one side of the fireplace was a large leather chair, and in front of it a narrow sofa, long enough for her to lie down on at full stretch, something which she had done often in the early days after her mother's death.

Was Dracco laying Lisa down on that sofa now, slowly, lovingly, longingly undressing her whilst she…?

Imogen gave a low, tortured moan of pure anguish.

She wanted to scream, to cry, to claw at her very flesh for so foolishly and wantonly betraying her, to tear her treacherous heart out of her body, to sear and seal her emotions so she would never feel again, but most of all she wanted to run as far and as fast away from Dracco as she could. Just as she had done once before.

But she wasn't a mere girl any more and answerable only to herself. She was a woman now, with responsibilities. Briefly, her hand brushed her stomach. A single tear rolled down her cheek. Imogen lifted her head.

She was Dracco's wife. He had married her of his own free will. She was carrying his child, their child. This house held so many precious happy memories for her of her life with her own parents. Her mother and her father. She fully intended that her child would enjoy the security of being loved by both its parents. No matter what the personal cost to herself.

And if that meant outfacing Lisa, standing her ground and claiming her rights as Dracco's wife, then that was exactly what she was going to do.

Lisa might have his love, but she was the one who would have his child!

CHAPTER EIGHT

'YOU'RE very quiet; is something wrong?'

'I was just thinking about the past and my father—and Lisa,' Imogen responded with deliberate emphasis, shaking her head as Dracco indicated the bottle of wine he had just opened.

She had visited her doctor earlier in the day and had had her pregnancy confirmed.

Whilst she suspected that the odd glass of red wine would not do her baby any harm, she was not prepared to take any risks. Already he or she was infinitely precious to her, and part of the reason she had been thinking about her father. He would have so loved being a grandfather, especially when Dracco, whom he had valued so much, was that baby's father.

But then, unlike her, her father had not known the truth about the man he had treated as a son. He had not known how Dracco had betrayed him with his own wife.

'Lisa never really loved my father. She only married him for his money.'

It must be the confirmation of her pregnancy that was making her feel so emotional, Imogen decided, that and the fact that her baby's father didn't love her. There had been another woman in the surgery at the same time as Imogen, very heavily pregnant and accompanied by her partner, who had watched her with such a look of tenderness and adoration that Imogen had felt her eyes sting. When the woman's hand had rested against her stomach he had lifted it to his lips, kissing it before replacing it on her belly and then covering it with his own.

'Lisa was a lot younger than your father, Imo.'

'Oh, of course you would take her side, wouldn't you?' Imogen stormed.

Dracco had been about to raise the glass of wine he had just poured himself to his lips, but now he put it down, frowning as he did so.

'I have no idea what all this is about, Imo,' he began austerely. 'You know—'

'I know that I saw Lisa here in this house and that you haven't said one word about her visit to me,' Imogen told him trenchantly.

'You saw her?' Dracco's frown deepened, his voice sharpening.

'Yes. What did you do, Dracco? Ring her up and tell her that it was safe to come over? That I was asleep? That you were tired of making love—oh, I'm sorry, having *sex*—with a woman you didn't really want and certainly didn't love? A woman who wasn't her? Well, this is my home, Dracco, and just so long as it is there is no way I intend to tolerate you entertaining your…your mistress in it…'

Imogen broke off and took a deep breath to steady her voice, but before she could continue Dracco was demanding tersely, 'What on earth are you talking about?'

Imogen couldn't believe his gall. It left her breathless, mute with a fury that visibly shook her body.

'You know perfectly well what I'm talking about,' she

threw at him when she could finally speak. 'I'm talking about the affair you are having with Lisa, the affair you were having with her when she was married to my father and which you have continued to have with her even though both of you have married elsewhere.'

She could see the muscles clenching in Dracco's jaw. He didn't like what she was saying—well, tough! How did he think she felt? How did he think her father would have felt?

'You think I'm having an affair with Lisa?'

He had to be working very hard to project such a convincing air of stunned disbelief, Imogen acknowledged, which just showed how important it was for him to keep his relationship with Lisa a secret.

'No, Dracco,' she told him calmly, 'I don't think you are having an affair with my stepmother; I know you are. Lisa told me so herself, on the morning of our wedding.'

There was a long, tense pause before Dracco asked grimly, 'Is that why you ran away?'

'What do *you* think?' Imogen responded bitterly, shaking her head before he could say anything else and telling him, 'That's it, Dracco. I'm not prepared to discuss it any further.' She felt amazed and awed by her own unexpected self-control—and the way she had taken charge of the whole situation. 'What's past is past, and it's the future that concerns me now. A future which you have forced on us both. I want to make it clear that I will not tolerate Lisa's presence here in this house. Not whilst I am expected to live here!'

Now she was going to tell him about the baby, their baby. And she was going to beg him, no, demand that he think about the effect his continued relationship with Lisa would have on the child he claimed he wanted so much! But before she could begin to speak the telephone suddenly rang.

Dracco turned away from her as he picked up the receiver, quite patently not wanting Imogen to overhear anything of the call. Because it was from Lisa? Suppressing her instinctive urge to wrench the phone from him and break the connection between them, Imogen turned instead and hurried into the hallway.

Where was her bravery now? she derided herself as she battled against her own emotions. Why wasn't she challenging Dracco? Was it because she was desperately afraid that she would lose, that he would choose Lisa above their baby?

There was no way she could allow herself to become the pathetic, unwanted, cheated-on wife of a man who found his pleasure with and gave his love to another woman, she reminded herself determinedly.

And if Dracco chose to ignore the demands she intended to make, the battle lines she intended to draw? Imogen could feel herself start to tremble. Her earlier buoyant surge of exhilaration had drained away, leaving her feeling afraid and vulnerable, not for herself but for her baby, who deserved surely to be loved by both its parents.

'Imo.'

She froze as Dracco came out into the hall and called her name.

'I've got to go to London, but when I come back there are things that you and I need to discuss, certain misconceptions you appear to have that need to be addressed and corrected.'

'I see. When will you be back?' She held her breath, even though she suspected she already knew the answer.

'I'm not sure.' Dracco's tone was cautious. 'I may have to stay overnight.'

May? Imogen only just managed to stop herself from laughing bitterly out loud. Even if the formality of his language hadn't been enough to tell her how furiously angry he was, the look on his face did, but Imogen had far more to concern her than Dracco's anger. Like, for instance, the source of that telephone call he had been so anxious for her not to overhear. It had to have been from Lisa! And now he was going to London to see her and no doubt spend the night with her!

She hated herself for not having the courage to challenge him. Was this what love did to you? Made you vulnerable? Afraid? Being unable to put her suspicions into words made her feel humiliated and ashamed.

Now, more than at any other time, surely, she ought to be able to turn to Dracco for his support and protection.

But she didn't seem to matter to him!

The sight of his own grim-faced expression as he glanced in his driving mirror only reinforced what Dracco already felt. It had stunned him to hear Imogen accusing him of having an affair with Lisa. Lisa might consider herself to be beautiful and desirable, but so far as Dracco was concerned she was ugly, ugly inside with malice, greed and selfishness. He had always suspected that Imogen's father had regretted marrying her, although he had been far too loyal to say so. His mouth tightened on the memory of the accusation Imogen had flung at him that he had been having an affair with Lisa whilst she was married to her father. Did Imogen really believe he was capable of that kind of disloyalty?

On the morning of their marriage when Imo had demanded to know if there was a woman in his life whom he loved he had assumed that she had been talking about herself. The horror and rejection in her voice and her eyes when he'd told her of his feelings had made him curse himself under his breath for what he had done to her.

The youthful infatuation she had had for him had quite plainly been destroyed by the unwanted reality of his love for her, a love which he had already been guiltily conscious she was really too young to be burdened with.

When she had run away from him that belief had been compounded. Dracco's eyes darkened with remembered pain. He had been on the verge of running after her when Henry had collapsed, and in the panic which had ensued everyone had automatically looked to him to take charge.

By the time he had been free to go after Imo it had been too late. She had already left the country.

He had tracked her down, of course, his concern for her as great as his searing anguish at losing her.

He had kept track of her ever since—for her sake and for what he owed her father. And it was for Imogen's sake that he was driving to London now, when he would far rather have been at home with her, explaining to her, reassuring her that Lisa was the last woman he would ever be interested in. Because there was and could only ever be one woman he loved and that woman was Imo herself.

However, his telephone call had been from the same agency he had used to keep track of Imogen during her absence, and they had rung to inform him as a matter of urgency that it looked as though the shelter was going to be closed down.

It seemed that the man who owned the building and the land on which the shelter stood wanted to sell the land on, and he was using strong-arms tactics to try to frighten the sisters into giving up their lease on the property.

Dracco knew just how much the shelter meant to Imogen, and he wanted to do everything he could to help save it, even if that meant helping to find and finance new premises for it.

He was driving to London so that he could, without Imogen discovering what was happening, negotiate some way of keeping the shelter open. No matter what it cost him.

Despairingly Imogen stood in the empty silence of the hallway. Dracco had left her to go to Lisa. What was she going to do?

She felt weak, defeated, frightened and alone. Her earlier confidence and bravado had completely left her. She desperately wanted to be with people who cared about her, people she felt secure with. Suddenly she missed Rio, and the sisters, the people she had known there—desperately.

What was going to happen to her and, more important, what was going to happen to her baby?

He or she needed to be loved. To be with people who cared—and for the right reasons!

Imogen knew exactly what she had to do!

This time there was no urgency, no sense of flight or desperation, just a chilling, calm acceptance of what had to be.

She packed carefully, and even managed to be controlled enough to ring ahead to Heathrow to book her seat on the first available flight to Rio.

It was leaving just before midnight, and she had plenty of time to get there.

Midnight. No doubt by then Dracco would be with Lisa in London at his apartment. In bed with her, no doubt, swearing eternal love to her.

Clutching her body, Imogen raced to the bathroom, her stomach churning with nausea.

'She has that effect on me too,' she comforted her still flat stomach sadly. 'He doesn't deserve you, my darling, no matter how much he wants you. I'm going to take us both somewhere we can be happy together without him.'

Even as she whispered the words to the new life growing inside her Imogen was aware of a small inner voice she couldn't quite silence that was objecting to what she was saying. It reminded her that although Dracco might not love her, that did not mean that he would not love his child, and that she had no real right to make decisions that would separate that child from Dracco forever.

She did not want to listen to that kind of criticism and she wasn't going to.

The taxi she had ordered arrived. She was travelling light—everything Dracco had bought for her, except this time her rings, she was leaving behind.

One small tear glittered in her eye as she closed the front door behind her. Refusing to look back, she got in the taxi.

Dracco grimaced, rubbing his hand over his tired eyes as he replaced the telephone receiver and switched on the computer on his desk.

He had managed, he hoped, to avert the crisis with the shelter—Dracco had managed to persuade the landowner to sell the shelter and the land to him, at a vastly inflated price, of course, but he didn't regret having to pay for it, not knowing how happy it would make Imogen. However, there were still certain ends he had to tie up, e-mails he had to send, people he had to contact—lawyers, accountants, bankers—but first…

He checked his watch; Imogen should still be up, and suddenly he desperately needed to hear her voice. He had hated having to leave her without talking through the whole ridiculous misunderstanding about Lisa, but he had felt that he needed time to explain everything properly to her. However, right now his need to speak to her was overwhelming everything else. He could at least tell her how much he loved her.

Dracco frowned. He had made three attempts to telephone Imogen without success. She could, of course, be asleep, or simply refusing to answer the telephone, but instinctively he knew that there was a more serious reason for her silence.

Without wasting time analysing his feelings, he reached for his car keys and headed for the door.

Heathrow was busy. Imogen had plenty of time before she needed to check in.

To distract herself from the pain of what she was having to do, she tried to make mental plans for the practicalities she would need to address once she arrived in Rio. Initially she would have to book into a hotel. Someone had now taken over her old apartment but even if they hadn't with a baby to consider she would have had to find somewhere more suitable to live, preferably a small house with its own garden.

She would also, no doubt, have to make arrangements to retain enough of the income from her share of the business to support herself and the baby, and perhaps even go back to teaching as well, instead of working full-time for the shelter.

At least there would be one advantage to her returning to Rio: her son or daughter would be bilingual. And yet for some reason, instead of making her smile, this recognition made her eyes fill with hot, acid tears.

It was nearly time to check in. Automatically she picked up her bag, and then realised that she needed to visit the ladies' cloakroom—a small side-effect of her pregnancy.

There was a little girl leaving the cloakroom at the same time as Imogen; blonde-haired and dressed in trendy denims, she appeared to be on her own, and instinctively Imogen kept a protective eye on her.

As they emerged onto the concourse the little girl ran towards a man who was standing several yards away.

Imogen could hear the love in her voice as she exclaimed, 'Daddy!' And she could see too the answering love in the man's eyes as he held tightly on to her, swinging her up into his arms.

'Come on, we'd better get you on your flight. If you

miss it your mother will never let you come and see me again.'

Now Imogen could hear pain and anger in his voice and, transfixed, she stood where she was watching them anxiously.

'I don't want to go back. I want to stay here with you,' the little girl was saying, and Imogen could hear the tears in her voice and see more in her father's eyes as he shook his head and started to carry her towards the departure gate.

Imogen felt as though she had been struck a mortal blow. One day would her child be like that little girl? Less than half a dozen yards away from her she could see another small family group, two adults—a man and a woman—and two children this time, two children with parents who loved them. Did she really want any less than that for her child?

If she went back to Rio now, and brought her child up alone, denying him or her to Dracco and denying him to them in return, what would her child ultimately think of her? Would he or she understand or would they blame her? Or, even worse in Imogen's eyes, would they simply suffer in silence, longing for the father they did not have?

She thought about the relationship she had had with her own parents, especially with her father. There was no way she could deny her child the right to have that magical, wonderful bond, to experience the love she had experienced. Dracco would love their child, his child; Imogen knew that instinctively. She took one step and then another, slowly at first, and then more quickly until she was almost running. She stopped only when the stitch in her side commanded her to, and her lungs were full of the sharp, acrid smell of the diesel fumes of the taxis outside the airport building.

It normally took two hours for Dracco to drive home from London—less when he did so late at night, but on this occasion he was unlucky. On this particular night an extra-wide load of dangerous chemicals was travelling along the motorway ahead of him at a speed which meant that it took Dracco over three hours to reach home.

When he did so he found the house in darkness and Imogen gone. Gone without any kind of explanation, any note.

Her hairbrush and a bottle of the perfume she always wore were still on her dressing-table. The perfume bottle had fallen over and Dracco could smell Imogen's familiar scent all around him.

He closed his eyes, his throat tight with emotion, raw with helpless anguish and fear. He could still see the look in her eyes when she had accused him of loving Lisa. Dear God, how could any woman be so blind? And how could any man be so stupid?

Why? Why hadn't he stopped to tell her the truth? Why the hell had he gone off like that, leaving her alone and vulnerable?

She believed him to be guilty of the worst kind of disloyalty, to her and to her father. And there were other issues at stake, such as the way he had treated her, the things he had said to her—and the things he hadn't said.

CHAPTER NINE

IMOGEN felt her heart starting to thump nervously as her taxi pulled into the drive. It was one in the morning, but all the house lights were on and Dracco's car was parked outside.

He had come back. He wasn't spending the night in London with Lisa!

As she got out of the taxi she had to fight against the feeling of dizziness filling her.

She was becoming used now to that disconcerting feeling of giddiness she sometimes experienced, especially when she first got up. But at least she wasn't actually being sick.

'You're a very good baby,' she whispered unsteadily to her stomach as she paid off the taxi and fought to hold on to her courage, 'a very good baby, and your mummy and your daddy are going to love you so very much.'

Had she been a fool to come back? From her own point of view, probably, she acknowledged as she opened the front door. But if Dracco dared to think that he could supplant her in her baby's life with Lisa then she was going to make sure he soon learned otherwise. She and the baby came as a package...a twosome, and if he wanted to make that a threesome then he had to take the pair of them together.

It was amazing, the strength and determination that

being a mother could give you, she acknowledged wryly as she came to an unsteady halt in the hallway, her heart pounding.

The study door started to open and Dracco came out. He looked as though he had undergone the most soul-destroying trauma. Dracco, whom she had never seen looking less than totally in control. His shirt was crumpled, and he needed a shave. His eyes were even slightly bloodshot!

Refusing to give in to the longing weakening her body, Imogen reminded herself of the decision she had just made and, drawing herself up, she fixed him with a look of angry distaste before demanding accusingly, 'I don't suppose I need to ask who you went to London to see?'

Dracco was looking at her with the kind of blank-eyed shock more appropriate, surely, to a man who had seen a ghost than one who had returned home from a rendezvous with his lover.

'Imo! You've come back. Oh, thank God, thank God!'

His voice sounded cracked, hoarse, and the look in his eyes as he strode towards her suddenly made her heart flip over inside her chest. Instinctively she backed away from him.

'I'm tired, Dracco,' she told him. 'I want to go to bed.'

'We need to talk.' He was insistent but Imogen shook her head. She knew she was far closer to emotional exhaustion than she dared to admit. If they started to talk now, to argue, she knew she wouldn't have the strength to say the things she wanted to say.

'No, not now,' she refused sharply. 'Not now, Dracco. Tomorrow.'

As much as he ached to beg her to listen to him, to find out where she had gone and why she had returned, to tell her how much he loved her and plead with her never, ever to leave him again, Dracco could see how vulnerable she was, and he wanted to protect her, to put her needs before his own.

'Very well,' he agreed heavily. 'But,' he told her, and, even though he gave her a wry smile, Imogen sensed that he meant it, 'I shall be locking all the doors and keeping the keys, Imo. So no more running away. I want you to promise me that.'

'I promise,' Imogen conceded tiredly as she headed for the stairs, praying that Dracco wouldn't make any attempt to follow her.

When he didn't, and when she finally closed the door of her old childhood bedroom behind her a part of her was weakly disappointed that he hadn't followed her. That he hadn't taken her in his arms and…and what? Face facts, she told herself wearily as she prepared for bed. Grow up, Imo. He doesn't love you. He loves Lisa.

'Can you answer that?' Imogen asked Dracco. 'I'm going to put the kettle on.'

Imogen had just arrived downstairs in the kitchen, having overslept, to find Dracco already there.

As he had said himself, they needed to talk, and the most important thing they had to talk about was the fact that she was carrying his child. Their baby!

Did she have the strength to concentrate on that all-important fact and to negotiate an acknowledgement from Dracco that their child had to come first—with both of them?

As he answered the phone Dracco kept on looking at Imogen, greedily, hungrily, absorbing the reality of her presence. He loved her so much!

What had happened? Why had she come back? Absorbed in his own thoughts, he took several seconds to realise what the caller on the other end of the telephone line was saying to him.

'Yes, I'll pass that message on to her,' he agreed quietly, his gaze still fixed on Imogen, who had turned away from the kettle to look at him.

He was watching her as though he had never seen her before, as though he was… Dizzy with the implausibility, the impossibility, surely, of what she seemed to be seeing in his eyes, Imogen stood still.

Silently Dracco replaced the receiver.

'What is it?' Imogen asked him uncertainly.

'That was the doctor's surgery,' Dracco announced with heavy quietness. 'They wanted to tell you that they've made an appointment for you at the hospital for your first antenatal clinic. You're pregnant with my child, and you didn't tell me!'

For the first time in her life Imogen did something she didn't think women did except in novels—she fainted!

When she came round she was lying on the sofa in the study, with Dracco leaning over her.

In the few seconds it had taken him to assimilate the information that Imogen was pregnant he had come from hope to despair as he recognised the reason why she had decided not to leave him. Imogen had her father's old-fashioned morals. She would not be able to leave him and take from him the child he had bargained with her to have. He had known that all along, and believed too that it would be impossible for her to leave her child either, which would mean that she would have to stay with him.

But now suddenly the realisation that she was here because she had conceived his child, rather than because she wanted to be, left a sour taste in his mouth.

Imogen shivered slightly, nervously aware of the way that Dracco was watching her and of the brooding, almost despairing look in his eyes. Because he had changed his mind? He didn't want a child by her any more?

'You're pregnant.' Dracco's voice was flat and empty of any expression for her to read.

'Yes,' she acknowledged. Please, God, don't let her cry, but this wasn't how such news should be broken—or received. So what had she expected, she challenged herself as her senses started to clear, a fanfare of trumpets proclaiming an ode to joy? Dracco gathering her up in his arms, his eyes full of tender worship and adoration?

Maybe that was unrealistic, but some expression of pleasure wouldn't have gone amiss, for their baby's sake if not for her own.

'Is that why you didn't leave—why you came back?'

'Yes,' she conceded as she swung her feet to the floor and then stood up. There was no way she intended to have this discussion with Dracco whilst in the disadvantageous position of lying down as he stood over her.

She intended to ensure that from now on whenever they met in the arena of conflict that she suspected wearily was going to be their marriage it was going to be on equal terms.

'I wanted to leave you, Dracco. You're having an affair with...with Lisa.' She stopped, her voice unsteady. 'But there was this little girl with her father, and suddenly I couldn't!'

Imogen turned away, but not before Dracco had seen the sheen of her tears in her eyes.

'Imo.'

Imogen tensed as Dracco grasped her hands in his, refusing to let her go, even though she tried desperately to pull away from him. She could feel his thumbs caressing the vulnerable undersides of her wrists in a way that sent hot shivers of pleasure racing up her arms.

'I don't know where you've got the idea that I'm having an affair with Lisa, but I can assure you that nothing could be further from the truth.'

That he could lie to her so uncaringly infuriated Imogen. Did he really think she was that much of a fool?

'No?' she challenged him. 'Then why did you go to London last night?'

Dracco shook his head, mentally cursing beneath his breath. Until everything was finally legalised, every 'i' dotted, every 't' crossed, he didn't want to tell her what had been going on, just in case something should go wrong.

'I can't tell you that, I'm afraid, Imo, but I can promise you that it wasn't to see Lisa.'

Imogen curled her lip in acid contempt as she pulled herself free of him.

'I don't believe you. Lisa told me on the morning of our wedding that you loved her. She challenged me to ask you about it. And she's confirmed her relationship with you to me since. I don't know which of you I despise the most. I suppose it must be you, if only because I never liked Lisa, whilst you…'

Imogen paused and then swallowed. What did it matter what she admitted to Dracco now about her past feelings for him? After all, she was pretty sure he must have known all about her foolish teenage crush on him.

Determinedly she looked up into his eyes and told him as calmly as she could, 'I adored you, Dracco. I put you up on a pedestal. I believed in you and I…' She stopped, appalled to discover how emotional she was becoming. 'After losing my parents, discovering how wrong I was about you was the most hurtful and traumatic thing I have ever experienced.'

She wasn't being totally honest with him, Imogen acknowledged as she looked away from him. The deaths of her mother and father had hurt, but after the immediacy of her shock and loss had worn off she had been left with the comforting knowledge that they had loved her.

In recognising Dracco's treachery she had been left with no such comfort whatsoever!

Dracco surveyed Imogen's downbent head for several seconds whilst he struggled to control the urgency of his longing to take her in his arms and hold her there until he had convinced her just how wrong she was.

'Do you really think I would have betrayed your father's trust like that?' he asked Imogen quietly.

'When love is involved other loyalties can sometimes cease to matter,' Imogen responded emptily.

Talking like this was stirring up so many painful memories inside her; too many.

'What I can't understand or forgive, Dracco, is that you were willing to marry me just for the sake of the business, even though you loved Lisa. And the way you lied to me about it… You did lie to me, didn't you?' she challenged him.

Dracco turned to stare out of the study window.

'Yes,' he admitted. 'I did. But not in the way that you think, Imo.' He heard her gasp and turned round just in time to see her almost running out of the room.

Oh, she was such a fool, Imogen derided herself as she hurried into the garden. She had to be to allow herself to still feel so much hurt over Dracco's behaviour towards her.

Instinctively she headed for her mother's rose garden, seeking its solace and comfort.

How could she possibly love a man who could so easily lie, and not just to her? Look at the way he had denied Lisa! Her hand stilled on the rose she had been touching.

What did she mean, love? She did not love Dracco.

Liar, a knowing inner voice taunted her. Of course you do; you've never stopped loving him and you never will!

'No!' A sharp pain slid through her heart. No, it couldn't be true. But of course she knew that it was.

Dracco frowned. Should he go after Imogen, make her listen whilst he tried to explain just how wrong she was and why? If he did, would she listen? He might have got what he had wanted for so long, Dracco acknowledged, but there was no real satisfaction in knowing that he was forcing Imogen to stay with him. Her presence in his life through force was not what he wanted; not in his life, or his bed. No, what he wanted was for her to be with him because she wanted to be, because she loved him.

His telephone rang and he went automatically to answer it, forcing himself to concentrate on what the client on the other end of the line was saying to him.

An unfamiliar car was coming up the drive, and Imogen shaded her eyes from the sun as it stopped and the driver got out. She smiled as she recognised David Bryant, Dracco's solicitor.

He was smiling back at her.

'How is your wife?' she asked him.

'Very pregnant and very hot.' He laughed. 'She hasn't got very long to go now, though. She wants Dracco to be one of the baby's godparents: she thinks the story of his love for you is very romantic.'

Imogen looked at him.

'I hope you don't mind me telling her,' he added uncertainly. 'My mother told me about it; she had heard it from my uncle. He thought a lot of Dracco, and of course Dracco consulted him after your father's death about what he should do. My uncle knew that your father made Dracco promise not to tell you about his feelings for you until you were over twenty-one. But he could see that your father's untimely death had changed things, and that you desperately needed someone in your life to protect you. According to my mother, my uncle fully endorsed Dracco's decision to ask you to marry him so that he could protect you and your inheritance.'

He avoided looking at Imogen as he continued, looking embarrassed, 'Of course, I don't know the whole situation—my mother has always maintained that you ran away because you were young and afraid, and suffering from young girl's wedding nerves—but it must have been hard for Dracco to lose you like that when he loved you so much.'

There was just the faintest hint of a gentle accusation in his voice.

'Still, at least it's all worked out well for you both now. My mother claims that she always knew that you'd be reconciled. Is Dracco in, by the way? I've got some papers for him to sign.' He was looking a bit self-conscious now, as though aware he'd said too much.

Her head was spinning with the shock of his revelations. Automatically she nodded and then watched as he walked towards the house. Then, very slowly and thoughtfully, she followed him.

Wearily Dracco got up from behind his desk. The house felt still and silent. Dracco had spent the hours since David Bryant had left thinking about the past—and the future—and questioning the role he had played in Imogen's life. Meanwhile he had mentally drawn up two tables, one listing the reasons why they should stay married and the other listing those why they shouldn't.

And from Imogen's point of view that list weighed heavily in favour of him setting her free, giving back to her the right to make her own decisions and choices.

He and Imogen needed to talk and there was no point in putting off what had to be said.

He found her upstairs in her old bedroom. She was sitting on the window seat with her knees drawn up into her body and her arms wrapped around them, a pose he remembered from her childhood.

Silently Imogen watched as Dracco came into her bedroom. She had come here after she had left the rose garden, moving like someone in a dream, needing somewhere safe to retreat to, somewhere she could examine and analyse her chaotic thoughts in peace.

David Bryant's comments had given her a tantalising glimpse into a situation she had never known existed; a situation, moreover, which totally changed her own interpretation of past events.

It wasn't hard for her to accept that her father would have guessed how she had felt about Dracco; after all, she had never tried to keep it a secret. But David's inference that Dracco had loved her and that her father had made him promise to keep that love a secret…

Ask him if there is a woman whom he loves, Lisa had challenged her on her wedding day, and she had done just that, and Dracco…

Could she have got it wrong, made a huge misjudgement and been encouraged to make it by Lisa? What if she had? What if the someone Dracco had loved had been not Lisa but her?

Her heart somersaulted and thudded so heavily against her chest wall that her whole body shook with the agitation of her emotions.

'Imogen.'

The sound of her full name on Dracco's lips when he

nearly always called her 'Imo' seemed somehow portentous.

She took a deep breath, her gaze searching his face, looking for some clue as to what he might be feeling, something to guide her, show her, but there was nothing. She would have to rely on her own intuition, her own need.

'Why did you marry me, Dracco?'

She could see that it wasn't the question he had been expecting. Even so, she noticed how he turned slightly away from her before he answered it, almost as though he didn't want her to be able to see his expression.

'You know why,' was his careful response.

'I certainly thought I knew why,' Imogen agreed quietly, getting off the window seat and coming to stand in front of him so that she could see his face. 'I was in the garden when David Bryant arrived. He told me…' She paused, wondering if she had the courage to go on. And then she thought of her baby, their baby, and knew that what she was doing wasn't just for herself, that it wasn't just her own future that was at stake, or her own happiness.

'Is it true that my father made you promise not to tell me you loved me until I was over twenty-one?' she challenged him.

At first she thought that he wasn't going to reply, and that alone was enough to make her heart start to hammer with fierce pleasure. After all, if what David had told her wasn't true then Dracco would have denied it immediately, wouldn't he?

'Is it, Dracco?' she persisted.

'Yes,' Dracco admitted tersely.

Dracco had loved her… Joy sang through her whole body, a glorious, empowering surge of deep female wonderment.

'Your father knew how I felt about you,' he told her. 'I couldn't have hidden it from him; it was hard enough hiding it from you, especially when…' He paused, his eyes dark and bleak, as though he was looking into a secret place that haunted him. 'He said that even though you had a teenage crush on me you were far too young to commit yourself to any kind of relationship with me, any kind of future. He said that such a relationship would be unfair to you, unbalanced, untenable, and that you needed time to grow up, to learn something of life and yourself.

'He knew that my feelings wouldn't change, but he was concerned that you should have the opportunity to change yours, and I agreed with him. Not that it was easy, not with you.' He broke off and shook his head. 'I ached for you so badly that sometimes…' He stopped. 'And then your father died.

'I didn't want to break my promise to him, but I had no choice. I talked to Henry about it, and he urged me to go ahead. He said that under the circumstances your father would have understood. You were only eighteen and so damned innocent; I knew that.' He stopped again. 'As it was, I hardly dared trust myself around you, but I had to honour at least part of my promise to your father. And so…'

'And so you planned for our marriage to be in name only,' Imogen supplied softly for him.

'Yes. I told myself that somehow I would find a way of waiting until you were twenty-one. You wanted to go to university. But then when we came out of the church you told me that you knew how I felt about you, and then…' he paused and looked directly at her '…then you ran away, leaving me in no doubt as to what you felt about being loved by me.'

'I didn't run away because you loved me, Dracco,' Imogen told him shakily. 'I ran away because I thought you loved someone else—Lisa. That was what she'd implied to me. She said there was someone in your life. She challenged me to ask you. If I had thought for one minute that you loved me then…'

'Then what?' Dracco asked her softly.

'Then.' Betrayingly Imogen's hand strayed towards her stomach as she tried to draw air into her lungs. 'Then right now this baby would probably be our third and not our first. Why didn't you tell me?' she demanded emotionally. 'You must have known how I felt about you.'

She ached for the years they had lost, the love she had gone without, the pain she had endured.

'You know why. I had promised your father, and I agreed with everything he had said. You were too young. I knew for your own sake I had to let you go. Not that I ever really did,' he admitted. 'I kept tabs on you the whole time you were in Rio, and when you came back—'

'You rejected me when I tried to tell you I loved you,' Imogen interrupted him sadly.

'Imo, I hated myself for the way I'd forced you into my bed, and because I wanted so much more from you than just sex. Too much more,' he groaned. 'Everything, all of you, just as I wanted you to accept and love all of me.'

She trembled wildly as he reached for her, allowing him to draw her into his arms, against his body.

'Kiss me, Dracco,' she demanded, lifting her face towards him, 'just to prove to me that this is really happening.'

Tenderly his lips brushed hers, but it wasn't enough for Imogen. She placed her hand on his jaw, maintaining the kiss, prolonging it, running her tongue-tip along the firm outline of his lips, tormenting and teasing them until Dracco gave a raw groan and gathered her even closer, close enough for her to feel his arousal.

'I felt so guilty about what I was doing,' Dracco admitted. 'I had forced you into a situation where you had no option other than to go to bed with me.' He stopped as he saw that Imogen was shaking her head.

'I could have refused if I'd really wanted to. Deep down inside it was what I wanted, you were what I wanted, even though initially I wouldn't admit it even to myself. That first morning after we'd made love...' she paused and shook her head in bemusement '...I felt as though finally my life was complete, Dracco, as though finally I was complete. But when I tried to tell you you rejected me, and then I remembered about Lisa.'

'Lisa never meant anything to me. I detested her both for the way she treated you and the way she abused your father's love.'

'She wanted you, though,' Imogen told him.

Dracco grimaced. 'Yes.'

Imogen waited. She knew that if he had tried to deny Lisa's desire for him she would have felt reluctant to trust him completely.

'She came on to me both during her marriage to your

father and afterwards, and I suspect that in implying to you that she and I...well, I suspect it was her way of hurting you and getting back at me. She knew how I felt about you. Although how on earth you could believe that I could ever be remotely interested in her...!'

One arm was holding her close to his side whilst his free hand lazily caressed her throat.

'She came here to see you,' Imogen pointed out.

'She gets biannual payments from your father's estate, and she wanted to try to persuade me to increase them. I told her that she was wasting her time. Just as we're wasting time now,' he whispered to her, adding, 'You don't know just how much I want to take you to bed.'

'Don't I?' Imogen teased him, moving closer to him with a small, blissful sigh as his hand cupped her breast, slowly kneading it whilst he started to kiss the soft, vulnerable flesh of her throat.

Tiny, delicious darts of pleasure rushed over her skin, making her shiver visibly and moan his name into the thick darkness of his hair. She could feel him drawing her towards her bedroom door.

'Right now, what I want more than anything I've ever wanted in the whole of my life is to lay you down on my bed, our bed, and...

'There's a bed in here,' Imogen reminded him, gesturing towards the narrow bed of her girlhood.

Immediately his eyes darkened. Shaking his head, he told her steadily, 'No...this room was yours as a child, Imo...a girl...and it isn't that child or that girl that I want to make love with now, much as I loved them both. It's you, the woman, my woman, I want to hold in my arms.'

As he very gently drew her through the bedroom door and closed it behind them Imogen felt her eyes smart slightly with tears.

Blinking them away, she touched his mouth with her fingertips. Soon now she would be kissing it, kissing him, touching him every way and being touched by him. As her breathing started to quicken with loving longing she suddenly remembered something.

'Well, if you weren't with Lisa last night, where exactly were you?'

The sombreness of his expression sent a tiny prickle of anxiety tingling down her spine.

Dracco took a deep breath. Now that David had brought the papers to him the future of the shelter was secure, and he could tell Imogen what had been happening without subjecting her to any anxiety. Very slowly he did so.

When he had finished she went quiet, and then Dracco saw the tears burning her eyes.

With a low groan he wrapped her in his arms, rocking her protectively.

'I shouldn't have told you. I've upset you and that's the last thing I wanted to do.'

'No, no, it isn't that,' Imogen reassured him shakily.

'Then what is it?' Dracco demanded.

'It's just knowing that you would do something like that for me, to make me happy. Me… You didn't know then about the baby.'

'Imo, there isn't anything I wouldn't do for you,' Dracco told her seriously, 'any sacrifice I wouldn't make.'

* * *

'Well, was it as good as you were expecting?' Dracco asked softly.

They had just woken up and Dracco was propped up on one elbow as he looked down at her.

Stretching luxuriously, revelling in the sensuality of his naked body next to her own, Imogen told him truthfully, 'No. It was even better...but just to make sure...'

As she traced the line of his jaw and reached up to kiss him Dracco groaned against her mouth.

'Come here, you wonderfully wanton woman,' he demanded as he wrapped his arms around her, 'my wonderfully wanton woman, my wife...my love...my life!'

EPILOGUE

'SHUSH...' Tenderly Imogen rocked her three-month-old son in her arms before turning proudly to listen to Dracco's short speech.

They had flown out to Rio early in the week, especially for the ceremony. Several of the sisters were crying openly as Dracco presented them with his cheque, and Imogen felt rather emotional herself, remembering just what he had done.

Alexander John had been less than three hours old when Dracco had come into her room at the hospital—the room that he had only left an hour earlier, having stayed with her throughout her labour—holding out to her an envelope, plus a small jeweller's box.

She had opened the box first, assuming that the envelope simply held a card, her eyes shining with shocked delight when she had seen the beautiful antique diamond ring Dracco had given her.

Whilst he'd slid it onto her finger he had told her, 'Before you open the envelope, let me tell you that it is not a gift from me to you, or even on account of you, infinitely beloved and precious though you are to me.'

Bemused, Imogen had waited.

'This is a gift on behalf of Alexander to those children who may not receive the love he is guaranteed.'

Imogen had been conscious of Dracco watching her

as she opened the envelope and removed the cheque inside it.

It had been made out to the shelter in Rio, and when Imogen had seen the amount of it her hand had trembled.

'Dracco…I know we made a bargain,' she had begun, 'but my feelings for you, our love…'

'You weren't listening properly to me,' he chided her gently. 'This has nothing to do with that, Imo. This is not so much payment of a debt but recognition of a gift. Your gift of love to me, mine to you, ours to our son, your father's to both of us.'

She had cried then, tears of joy and love and gratitude for everything she had been given, but most of all for Dracco himself and for their child.

And now here she was, watching as Dracco formally handed over his cheque to Sister Maria.

She had been talking to one of her old colleagues, who had informed her that it was only thanks to Dracco's timely intervention that the shelter had been saved. They all thought that he was wonderful and that she was very lucky to be married to him, and Imogen fully agreed! In her arms, Alexander gurgled and smiled up at her. Hugging him, she kissed him. He was the image of Dracco, apart from the fact that he had her father's nose.

Dracco, his speech over, was walking towards her. Imogen smiled lovingly at him. Suddenly she couldn't wait for them to be alone together.

As though he had guessed what she was thinking as he reached her, Dracco drew her into his side, bending his head to kiss her. The love in his eyes as he looked at her made her heart flood with joy. He was everything she had ever wanted and everything she would ever want.

'I love you,' she whispered emotionally to him as he released her mouth.

'I love you too, Imo,' he responded tenderly. 'I always have and I always will.'

Coming Next Month

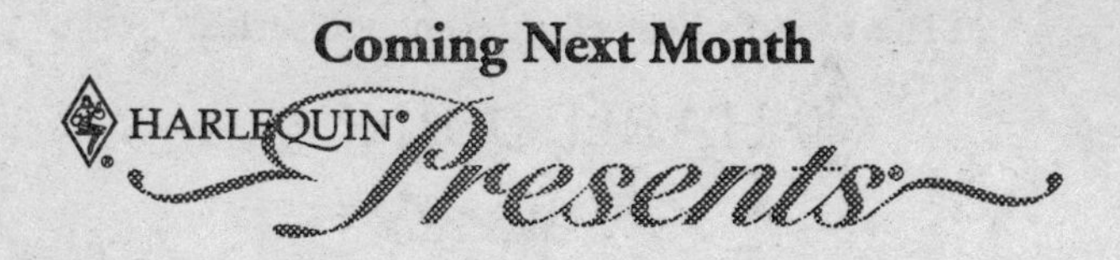

THE BEST HAS JUST GOTTEN BETTER!

#2253 THE ARRANGED MARRIAGE Emma Darcy
Alex King is the eldest grandson of a prestigious family—and it's his duty to expand the King empire. He must find a bride and then father a son. Alex thinks he's made the right choice, so why is his grandmother so eager to change his mind?

#2254 THE SHEIKH'S CHOSEN WIFE Michelle Reid
Leona misses her arrogant, passionate husband, Sheikh Hassan ben Al-Qadim, very much. She'd left him after she'd been unable to give him the heir he needed. But a year later Hassan tricks her into returning....

#2255 THE GREEK TYCOON'S BRIDE Helen Brooks
Andreas Karydis had women falling at his feet, so Sophy was determined not be another notch in his bedpost. But he doesn't want her as his mistress—he wants her as his English bride!

#2256 THE MISTRESS SCANDAL Kim Lawrence
Ally didn't regret her one night of passion with Gabe MacAllister and had never forgotten it. She was reminded every time she looked at her baby son. Then three years later, Ally is stunned to discover that Gabe is the brother of her sister's new fiancé!

#2257 EXPECTING HIS BABY Sandra Field
Lise knew all about ruthless airline tycoon Judd Harwood—but he needed a nanny for his daughter, Emmy, and against her better judgment Lise took the job. She never intended to spend a night of blazing passion in his bed!

#2258 THE PLAYBOY'S PROPOSAL Amanda Browning
Joel Kendrick was the sexiest man Kathryn had ever met. Never one to refuse a challenge, she flirted back when Joel flirted with her! But flirting turned to desire on Joel's part—and true love on Kathryn's....

HPCNM0502